THE PIE IN THE SCRY

SHADY GROVE PSYCHIC MYSTERIES, BOOK 5

ADA BELL

EMPRESS BOOKS

THERE'S A KILLER ON THE LOOSE, AND THEY LOOK LIKE ALY

Aly's used to getting visions by now, but she never expected to see herself murdering the town's beloved yet crotchety baker. Obviously, that never happened. Then the police arrive at her house with a warrant. If she didn't kill Tony, why does she have his baker's hat?

When Aly finds herself reliving the same day over and over, things go from strange to supernatural. Where did that vision come from? Aly's never seen the future before—only the past. At first she thinks the vision was a trick, sent as a distraction by the same person who killed her sister-in-law. But as she works to stop them, Aly discovers that her vision of Tony might not have been a lie so much as a premonition.

ALSO BY ADA BELL

Shady Grove Psychic Mysteries

Mystic Pieces

The Scry's the Limit

Sight Seeing

Mystic Treasure (Book 3.5)

Seer Today, Gone Tomorrow

The Pie in the Scry

Mystic Persons

✶ Created with Vellum

To Katrina

Thanks for letting me "borrow" your name.
Sorry I killed you.

CHAPTER ONE

MONTHS OF STUDY and meditation and preparation had led to this moment. The tower of magic ingredients covered the checkout counter and went up from there, extending until I needed to stand on tiptoes to meet Amira's eyes. Some would say I'd gone a wee bit overboard in purchasing supplies for tomorrow's spell. Luckily, none of those people were here.

"Do you think it's enough?" I asked. This spell was so important. I didn't want to leave anything to chance. Everything had to go perfectly. Which was why I'd accepted my brother's credit card before going shopping. Only the best to save our family.

My friend and owner of the magic store lifted one eyebrow skeptically. I'd always wanted to learn to do that. "Honey, you've got everything here and the kitchen sink. We've gone over and over the spell. You've got a comprehensive list of ingredients—and also, I own a magic shop. I can bring anything else you might need with me tomorrow. Or I would have been able to if you hadn't cleaned me out."

As if agreeing with her, the overhead lights flickered.

"Adding ambiance?" I asked skeptically.

"Oh, that's my ghost. I mean, I think I have a ghost."

My ears perked up. Shady Grove was a place where the fantastic sometimes became the mundane. Although rumor said the local bar was haunted, I hadn't seen a ghost since moving here. That was despite encountering psychics, witches, and my boyfriend Sam, who I still thought might be an empath.

"You have a ghost? That's so cool! Who is it?"

"I don't actually know. He hasn't introduced himself yet," she admitted. "But I'm sure it's just a matter of time. He—or she—has been playing with the lights for a few days now."

My eyes went over the pile of supplies again. Then I turned to examine the rest of the store, desperately seeking anything we might have missed. Like most of the buildings on Main Street, this one was centuries old and had immense character. Amira had hung tapestries on the walls, added gauzy curtains to the large plate-glass windows leading outside, and replaced the door to the back room with strings of beads. Soothing music played over the speaker system, and she burned a stick of incense to complete the effect.

I inhaled deeply, letting the sandalwood seep into my bones. After holding my breath and counting to four, I released it. The breathing technique worked for half a second. "Do you think we need more candles?"

"Stop fussing! We've got this."

Two years ago, my sister-in-law was murdered. It had taken me almost a year to prove it, but finally, I was sure: Katrina was killed by her sister Mary. A few weeks ago, Kevin and I had worked out a plan. He took my four-year-old nephew Kyle to Boston for the weekend to get him out of the way. Amira's mother, a powerful witch, went along to protect them. Tomorrow Amira and I, along with my friend Emma, would lure the murderer to us, bind her powers, force her to confess to killing Katrina, and turn her over to the police.

At least, that was the plan. Part of me worried we wouldn't be able to pull it off. Emma only came into her magic last summer. But this was it. Mary had been making life increasingly difficult ever since I discovered my psychic powers. Tomorrow was the anniversary of Katrina's death, our best chance of tapping the energy required to do the spell. We needed to stop Mary before she hurt anyone else.

"Aly? Are you still with me?" Amira asked teasingly.

Finally, I pulled Kevin's credit card out of my wallet and handed it over.

To take my mind off my nerves, I asked, "What are your plans for today? Going dancing with your ghost?"

"Not today. I'm actually going to look at a house for sale."

"Amira! Are you moving?" Since I'd met her, she'd lived with her parents next door to me and Kevin. While I got not wanting to live with your parents at twenty-six, having her nearby comforted me.

She nodded while loading my purchases into my reusable cloth bags. "I think so, maybe. It's time. Don't worry, I'm not going far."

"Of course you're not. Shady Grove doesn't have 'far.'"

The entire town covered about four square miles. Our population was less than ten thousand people, and we basically had three housing developments. Not a ton of options around here.

"The realtor I'm working with has listings in Shady Grove and Willow Falls." Her cheeks turned red at the mention of him. For the first time, I noticed she was wearing more make-up than usual. Her hair was carefully styled and curled. Her red sweater highlighted her features nicely, and its v-neck hinted at more cleavage than she normally revealed while working at I'll Put a Spell on You.

"You're holding out on me," I said. "Do you have a date with the realtor?"

"Sort of. Okay, no. I mean, I hope he'll ask me out. He's really cute."

The lights flickered again.

"That's my cue to stop talking," she said. "My ghost is getting jealous."

"If you're going to take social cues from a spirit, you really should name him," I pointed out. "Casper? Beetlejuice?"

She snorted as the lights flickered again. "Look, even the ghost hates that idea. Do you need help getting to your car?"

"I love that you've given a malfunctioning lightbulb a personality," I said. "Thank you so much. Good luck with your not-a-date, and I'll see you tomorrow."

"Have a good evening," she said with a broad smile. "And Aly? Don't worry. We're ready. We haven't left anything to chance."

After loading up my trunk, I dropped by Missing Pieces, the antique store about half a block down Main Street. My boss and mentor Olive was there, and she was holding onto one last item we needed to make the spell work.

Two years ago, my brother Kevin and his wife, Katrina, had been living happily in a McMansion in a fancy New York City suburb. Kevin worked about six hundred hours a week for this huge law firm and got paid buckets of money. Like, Scrooge McDuck buckets. Then, one day, he came home from work to find his wife dead. The house was locked. There were no witnesses, no suspects, but signs of a struggle. Police spent several months investigating, but they never turned up any real leads.

Finally, they'd been forced to admit they had no idea what had happened, and the case went onto the list of unsolved murders.

Until I'd moved to Shady Grove.

On my twenty-first birthday, I'd discovered the power to see flashes of the past when using certain objects. Just holding an item was rarely enough, an irritating fact when trying to read from things like a child-sized rocking horse. But for the most part, I'd learned to use my powers, even teaching myself to scry in a mirror for visions when I didn't have an object related to the person or place I wanted to view.

After learning about my psychic powers, I'd devoted myself to finding out what happened to Katrina so we could bring her killer to justice. Kyle deserved to know the truth about his mother, and Kevin would never fully move on without getting answers.

Since I'd started digging, Kev finally seemed to be coming to terms with losing Katrina. He looked more relaxed, lighter. I suspected that once he got justice, he'd finally be comfortable taking the next step with his girlfriend, Julie. It had been more than a year before he'd even considered starting dating again, but the two of them really complemented each other. As much as I loved Katrina, it was time for Kevin to put her to rest.

My brother deserved to be happy. Since he'd given me a home, I wanted to give back as much as possible. I owed him —if I hadn't moved here, I never would have met Olive or Sam. My Shady Grove family meant everything to me.

Olive returned from the back storage room and held out a shiny crystal orb. It shimmered as if lightning moved beneath the surface. The first time I'd seen it, I'd expected to be zapped, but something about it felt oddly comforting. Like it was meant to be with me. Or more accurately, us. The orb belonged to Kevin and Kyle. Katrina made it for them before she died and hid it with a friend until the right time. That time was now.

"Are you sure you don't want me to keep it one more night?" she asked.

I shook my head. "If Mary does any readings on the house, I want her to sense its power and think Kyle is home with me. The last thing we need is for her to realize Kevin took him away, ignore our bait, and follow them to Boston."

"A wise choice." She took in my tense shoulders, the dark shadows under my eyes. Although a psychic and not an empath, Olive missed nothing. I didn't need to tell her that fears of messing up this spell kept me tossing and turning at night. "Everything is going to work out, Aly. We're ready."

I hesitated. "What if it's not enough? What if I'm not enough? I'm not a witch, I'm a psychic."

Sure, I'd been working hard for almost a year now. My progress generally made me happy, but being able to read psychic impressions from objects was still a far cry from the type of spell we'd worked out for tomorrow.

She took my hand and held my gaze. "Rajini Patel tailor-made this spell for us. For *you*. She knows your power and she knows her daughter's. Between Amira and Emma, you've got the strength to work it. All three of us will be there for support. If all that doesn't make you feel better, this orb is your secret weapon."

"I guess. I'd just feel better if we could do it now and get it over with."

"I know you would, dear, but since we're using Katrina's essence, doing the spell on the anniversary of her death is going to give us the best possible chance of success."

Olive was right. She was always right, a fact that was sometimes infuriating but now comforted me. "I know, I know."

"Everything is going to be fine," Olive emphasized. "Go home. Have a lovely afternoon resting. Stop worrying."

Her certainty lifted me on the way back to the car. We'd planned and prepared. We'd made our trap. Tomorrow we were going to lure Mary right into it. Nothing could stop us now.

CHAPTER TWO

BEFORE HEADING HOME, I had one final stop to make. A few blocks from Main Street sat a bakery with such amazing baked goods, sometimes I wondered if the owner also possessed magical powers. Despite being off the strip and therefore exempt from the town's kitschy business name requirements, he'd decided to go with the flow and name the place Let's Bake a Deal. Once I met the guy, that made no sense, but I still appreciated the gesture.

All the way from my car to the front door, I prayed Tony would be out sick and his sister running the shop in his absence. Donna was a delight. Always chatting and making people feel at home. Tony was… Well, let's just say he was lucky his cupcakes tasted like Zeus infused them with ambrosia.

The door swung open, ushering me into a glorious haven of sugar and icing and vanilla and chocolate and—

"You." Behind the counter, Tony pointed one finger at me without a trace of a smile on his face. "What do you want?"

It took every ounce of restraint I possessed not to tell him I wanted a bakery with someone who possessed an iota of customer service skills. He'd toss me out, and I'd have to go all the way to Willow Falls to get a dessert to share with Sam tomorrow. Or worse, a stale apple pie from Patti's Diner. No, thanks.

I forced a smile onto my face. "It's good to see you, too, Tony. What are the daily specials?"

"The specials are for *paying customers.*"

"One time. One time, I asked if you were willing to negotiate. That was two years ago." Trying not to roll my eyes, I pulled out my wallet. A piece of paper fluttered to the ground, but I kept my focus on Tony. "Look. I have monies."

"Decide fast. I don't got all day."

"Such a sweet talker. Save some of the sugar for the cupcakes, Tony."

He put his hands on his hips. "You want something or not?"

The unfortunate answer was yes. Yes, I did. Seriously, there had to be something in these cupcakes to keep us coming back. I should buy an extra and take it to the science lab on campus to run some experiments.

"Yes, please," I said through gritted teeth. "Do you have any special flavors today?"

"All my flavors are special, kid. Pick one or go."

My phone rang. Oh, no. Tony hated cell phones. He had a massive sign on the wall forbidding them in the shop, but I'd forgotten to turn mine off before walking in. I couldn't answer it. I couldn't take it out of my bag to silence it. Maybe I'd get lucky, and he wouldn't hear it.

"What's that noise?"

"Um...it's just me singing," I said. "Shake it off! Shake it off!"

Tony shook his head. "Are you on drugs? Get out of my shop!"

"No! I'm sorry. Look, Tony, I really need some cupcakes.

My boyfriend is coming to town tomorrow. I'll take whatever you've got. Anything but lemon."

"Today's special is lemon meringue."

"You're making that up," I said.

"Take it or leave it." My phone rang again, filling the air with the ringtone I'd recently assigned to Kevin. Tony pointed at a sign behind the register. "On second thought, just leave it. No phones in my bakery. That's your third strike."

With no better way to quiet the thing quickly, I hid my bag behind my back. "What? This isn't baseball. Look, I can't control my phone ringing."

"Not my problem. Like I said, you gotta go. If you leave right now, I might sell to you next time you come in."

This was ridiculous. Sure, Tony wasn't the nicest guy around, but something was making him worse than usual. Although I desperately wanted to tell him I would never ever come back, I was a terrible baker who really liked cupcakes. So I swallowed back a biting retort that would get me banned forever, shoved my wallet back into my bag, and turned toward the exit.

Flinging the door open, I stormed out of the bakery. I barely made it to the sidewalk before letting out a frustrated scream.

"Is everything okay?"

The voice made me jump. I'd been so irritated, I hadn't even realized anyone else was around. Sheriff Matthews stood there, looking at me with his inquisitive dark eyes.

Great. He didn't like me any more than Tony did. If there were an Aly anti-fan club, those two would be co-Presidents. Shady Grove's highest law enforcement officer—and one of exactly two who worked full time for the force—was a sturdy black man who stood close to six feet tall with broad shoulders and an intimidating glare. Gray streaks were starting to sneak into his goatee and near his temples. He always wore his uniform, whether sitting behind his desk or at the bowling alley on a Friday night. I probably wouldn't recognize him if he showed up somewhere without it.

If I were polite, he should let me go about my day without hassling me.

"Everything's fine, Sheriff," I said. "How are you?"

Ignoring my question, he asked, "Is Tony out of baked goods?"

It took a minute for me to understand what he was asking. "Oh, I was just browsing."

He chuckled and patted his belly, which was pretty flat from my perspective. "Browsing? You've got more willpower than I do."

This was probably the longest, most civil conversation I'd had with Sheriff Matthews since he'd accused Olive of murder earlier this year. Must be almost election time if he was even stopping to chat with me, of all people. He hadn't been very pleased when I'd discovered the real murderer.

Perhaps if he'd been willing to spend more time investigating and less time being the Mayor's lapdog, I wouldn't have made him feel so silly. Ah, well. That was in the past, and I had a trunk full of magic supplies to get home and unpack.

"I forgot my wallet," I lied, then instantly regretted it. If he talked to Tony, he'd know I'd been waving it around. That's what happened when I got flustered. Ridiculous how the sheriff always managed to make me feel like I was doing something wrong.

A walkie-talkie on his hip crackled, and instantly, he grabbed it. "Sheriff here. Over."

"Sheriff, this is the Little [static]. We've got a situation [static] in my pants. Over."

My lips twitched. For quite a while, Sheriff Matthews had been having a not-so-secret affair with one of the town's married residents. Either she'd decided to go public, or she'd expected him to be alone. They must be on a private channel. Either way, I'd heard more than I needed to know.

Sheriff Matthews glowered at me, which helped me wipe away my amusement. "You need something, girl?"

Averting my gaze, I yanked my own phone out of my bag. "Nope. I'm good. Gotta go! Enjoy the baked goods, Sheriff."

Now that I was holding my phone, I should call Kevin back. Since Sheriff Matthews was still giving me the hairy eyeball, the second my brother answered, I cut him off.

"Is everything okay? What's the emergency? Is Kyle hurt? I'm on my way!"

"Um, Kyle is fine. Sleeping in the backseat of my car, thanks to the magical songs of *Daniel Tiger's Neighborhood*." Understandably, my brother sounded confused. "Are you okay? Listen, if you're in trouble, I want you to repeat after me: Please only address me as Aluminum from now on."

"Very funny, Kelvy." Our science-loving parents inexplicably named my older brother after their favorite unit of temperature and me after the thirteenth element. It had become a running joke between us, but really, I was just grateful not to be called Celsius. Kevin got a name change when he turned eighteen, but "Aly" suited me nicely. Sliding into the front seat of my Prius, I risked a glance back at the bakery. Sheriff Matthews had paused between two buildings to talk to his girlfriend. "Just trying to avoid a weird conversation with the sheriff."

"What was weird about it?"

"He was being nice to me." I thought for a minute. "Do you think Tim Matthews needs a science tutor? Does he have any kids?"

"Nah. Maybe he finally realized that Shady Grove is a better place thanks to you doing half his job."

"In that case, he should pay me a commission," I said as I got into my car. "Anyway, we're all set for tomorrow. I just picked up everything except the cupcakes I wanted."

"I keep telling you to be nicer to Tony."

"Today was not my fault. Something is definitely bugging that guy," I said. Then I sighed. "Okay, maybe I'm a little on edge."

"Are you sure you don't want me to help?"

"No." I shook my head, although he couldn't see me. "We don't know what could happen if the spell goes wrong. If this backfires, I don't want you or Kyle within a hundred miles of Shady Grove."

"Okay, *Mom.*"

"You know I'm right. Which reminds me—can you call when you get to the hotel? I'll feel better knowing that you checked in without any surprises from Mary," I said.

Normally, that sort of over-protectiveness would drive Kevin up the wall. But we'd been through a lot this year. After working endlessly the past few months to perfect our plan to stop Mary and keep Kyle safe, both of us preferred the reassurance.

"Sure. And if you decide to try to get yourself killed before tomorrow, give me a heads up, please," my brother replied.

Kevin didn't like me putting myself into dangerous situations to solve crimes. It was one of the few things we disagreed on. I didn't like danger either, but I'd been granted this gift, and I felt like I had an obligation to use it to make the world a better place. Like finding murderers.

My brother didn't disagree, per se, but he preferred I just figure out who the bad guys were and point the police at them. If only they believed in psychics, I'd be happy to oblige.

"I shall do everything in my power to stay alive. Pinky swear," I said. "Give Kyle hugs and kisses from me when you stop. And maybe a doughnut."

"Yes, I'll be sure to give my four-year-old a doughnut before bed, plus an espresso and that puppy he's always wanted." The amusement in Kevin's voice carried clearly through the phone. "Listen, traffic is getting heavy. I'll text you when we're settled."

I thanked him and hung up the phone, hoping that by the time I saw my brother again, Mary would be one hundred percent in the rearview mirror.

FOR THE REST of the drive home, I thought about all the things I could do alone in the house for two days. Walking around with no pants. Eating an entire batch of chocolate chip cookie dough without having to bake any cookies—or worse, share. Spend some time with my boyfriend without being interrupted by a four-year-old. Do a quick locating spell to track down Mary and bind her powers so I could take her to the police.

The perfect weekend.

This was the first time I'd be sleeping alone in the house since moving in over two years ago. Sam lived in New York City while he worked on his M.B.A., but he planned to drive up tomorrow morning to spend the day with me. To celebrate if the spell went right or comfort me if... No. To celebrate.

Leaving me about eight hours to relax, prepare a bath, and get started on that cookie dough while snuggling on the couch with Kyle's pet turtle, Mercury. I'd already bought a big tub of the stuff to avoid the hassle of having to put ingredients together in a way that wouldn't poison me.

This had to work. We'd been through so much the past two years. Katrina's death had dominated our lives for so long. Once we brought her killer to justice, we could all start the next chapter.

These thoughts consumed me until I pulled my car into its spot in the garage and braced myself to open the door.

To say Shady Grove got cold in February was like saying Sue Grafton wrote "a few books." The temperature had gotten just high enough to melt some of the snow on the front walkway before refreezing, which created a lovely skating rink between the driveway and our house. Since I didn't want Sam to slip and fall, I grabbed the bag of salt Kevin had left and got to work. Our driveway wasn't huge, but the air outside was coooooold. By the time I finished, I was asking myself why I ever left California.

My packages from the magic store could stay in the trunk until I no longer resembled a popsicle. For now, I moved into the house, rubbing my hands up and down my arms. By the time I dug the cookie dough out of its hiding place under the broccoli, I finally felt human.

I was halfway through taking off my coat when the door-bell rang.

The sound made me jump. Sam wasn't due until tomorrow morning. I glanced at the clock. 2:57 p.m. Our mail usually arrived earlier, but I hadn't checked the box on my way in. It could be a package.

Maybe Mr. Patel came over to give me some news from his wife or to borrow some salt? Now I was glad I'd taken the time to do the driveway. The last thing I needed was to injure my next-door neighbor or some kid going door-to-door selling candy for school sports.

On my way down the front hall, I tried to peer through the window by the door. I didn't see anyone, so that meant probably a delivery. Our subscribe and save order wasn't due until next week, but Kevin could've forgotten to mention he was expecting something else. After hanging my jacket on the hook in the front hall, I opened the door.

As suspected, no one stood there. There weren't any cars in the driveway or on the street. At my feet, a cardboard box sat on the doormat. The rest of our mail lay on top of it, saving me a trip to the end of the driveway later.

Leaning down, I picked everything up. A few envelopes and one parcel. The package looked completely normal. A standard U.S. Priority Mail medium-sized box, just like my mom used whenever mailing us gifts. And by "us," I mostly meant Kyle. The return address was hard to read, but that's what she got for insisting on using those fancy pens that smeared.

The rest of the mail went straight into the recycling bin set in the hallway for that purpose: meal kit offers, ads, *Highlights Kids* for Kyle. Wait. I fished that one out and set it on the entry table. Then I shut the front door against the cold and examined the box in my hands.

"Aly Reynolds."

Hold up. Mom—despite a lifetime of protests—still insisted on calling me Aluminum. She put it on every single package she sent. The thought had barely flitted through my mind before I finished opening the box. At first glance, it was empty. Then I shook it. A piece of white cloth fell out, neatly folded.

My nose wrinkled at the faint smell of burnt sugar. Who would send me dirty laundry? Gingerly, I unfolded it and shook it out. A chef's hat. Huh. I left it on the table for a sec and poked my fingers into the box looking for a note, a packing slip, a gift receipt. An awful gift, but still. Nothing.

I flipped it over, this time taking a good look at the front. Just my name, written with block letters in somewhat smeared black ink. The return address was illegible, which now seemed less careless and more intentional. How dumb to assume this box came from my mother. I should have known something was up.

There was no postage on the box. This might be intended

to be U.S. Priority mail, but it hadn't been delivered by the postal service. No FedEx or UPS markings, either. I didn't know if they would even allow someone to use a competitor's box, but it didn't matter. This box hadn't gone through a shipping service's system. It must have been hand-delivered.

I opened the door and craned my neck outside, but no one was there. The path to the front door was clear enough not to show footprints, and if anyone had parked in the driveway, they were gone now. I hadn't noticed tire marks other than my own, but I hadn't been looking for them.

Who would leave a chef's hat on my porch? And why?

Shady Grove was a small town. We had about ten thousand residents, a coffee shop, and a diner. No real restaurants: you had to drive over to Willow Falls if you wanted a fancy sit-down meal. My next-door neighbor, Mr. Patel, owned a delicious Indian place over there, but if he wanted to give me a chef's hat... Actually, he would not want to give me a used chef's hat. He'd find it unsanitary.

He'd be right.

I couldn't think of a single reason Patti from the diner or Tony would want to give me a chef's hat, and Julie didn't wear one at the coffee shop.

Maybe this wasn't intended for me at all? A wrong address? Seemed unlikely, since no one else had a name like mine, but stranger things had happened.

I ran my fingers over the fabric, looking for anything to give an indication of ownership. A name tag, a stray hair, anything. Finally, with a shrug, I put the hat atop my head. I barely had a moment to note how cute I looked in the mirror over the hall table before the world vanished.

Someone shoved me, hard. I staggered backward, waving my arms. What was going on? To catch my balance, I grabbed the edge of a nearby counter. Where was I? The hands gripping the smooth metal possessed hairy knuckles and blunt fingernails. A dark, natural olive skin tone. A glimpse of tile beneath my shoes suggested I was in a kitchen, maybe? A huge kitchen.

Then I spotted the name tag on my white coat. A chef's coat, bearing the name "Tony". Okay, so I was at Let's Bake a Deal. When? Was this earlier today? Maybe Tony was in a terrible mood when I dropped by because something had happened to him earlier.

While I struggled to center myself, the person I found myself inhabiting surged forward, racing toward... Me? I stood there. I mean, not me Tony, but me Aly. Shoulder-length chestnut brown hair. Brown eyes. Pale face, with a smattering of freckles across her nose. My nose? Vague resemblance to Anna Kendrick, or so I liked to tell myself.

While I gaped at my own face, a brown cylindrical object whizzed through the air toward my...other face? Tony's face. This was so weird.

That last thought barely registered when something whacked me on the side of the head. The last thing I saw was my own face staring back at me. Then everything went black.

Gasping for air, I yanked the hat off my head.

What was going on? I'd never been in Tony's kitchen and couldn't think of any reason for going there. He certainly wasn't going to invite me.

I also would never hit Tony with a... What was that? Some fancy kitchen thingamajig. Whatever it was, I'd never used one. Didn't know if we had one. So how did I get it and why would I brandish it around like a weapon?

Didn't matter. I wouldn't hit Tony, no matter how much I disliked him.

This was so bizarre. Never had I experienced a vision of the future. My visions came from the past. The scene I'd just witnessed never happened. I might have wanted to chuck something at him earlier, but I didn't.

Had I been mistaken? The girl in the vision looked like me, sure. No. I saw that face in the mirror every day for the past twenty-one years, eleven months. It was me. I just didn't know how I wound up in a vision of someone attacking Tony.

When did this happen? Maybe it was an old vision. I hadn't seen Tony's face. Maybe someone who looked like me used to live in Shady Grove and killed a different baker? Someone also named Tony? Yes, I was grasping at straws, but nothing made sense.

I should call Olive. Or go to the bakery. Nah. No way to know how Tony would react to me having his chef's hat. He'd either agree to sell me a cupcake for returning it or stuff me into one of his ovens. I sincerely doubted he'd talk to me about the time he got hit in the face by someone who looked like me in his kitchen.

A pounding on the door jolted me back to the present. The house shook from the force. A deep voice boomed through the wood.

"Aluminum Reynolds! This is the police. Come out with your hands up!"

CHAPTER FOUR

THE BANGING FISTS and loud voice made me jump. Confusion nailed me to the spot. What was happening? Was Tony okay? And if he wasn't, why would anyone come looking for me?

Quickly, I reviewed what I knew: Sheriff Matthews had seen me in front of the bakery earlier today. I'd had a vision showing something terrible happening to Tony. His baker's hat was now in my possession.

Police were standing on my front doorstep. They were banging on the door, telling me to come out with my hands up. That wasn't how the police approached someone if they just had a few questions for a potential witness. That's how police treated suspects.

Sheriff Matthews *saw* me leaving Let's Bake a Deal. When I was agitated. And now a hat told me something happened to Tony right before the sheriff showed up on my doorstep. That couldn't be a coincidence.

Someone banged on the door again. "If you're in there, it'll be better to open up now."

He'd once arrested Olive for a crime she didn't commit with less evidence. He'd never believe that Tony was coincidentally killed by someone who looked exactly like me, then left his hat on my doorstep.

At that thought, my "fight or flight" reflex kicked into overdrive. I couldn't fight the police, but I could get out of here. I turned and ran for the back door.

Although the sheriff hated me, his nephew Doug and I had a pretty decent relationship. After a rocky start, we put our differences aside when he began dating my best friend. Also after I promised to never steal evidence from a crime scene again. Which, in my defense, only happened once. That thought had me looking guiltily at the chef's hat still clenched in one hand. Not the same, though! I didn't steal this. Someone mailed it to me.

I hadn't gone anywhere near a crime scene, as far as I knew.

The hat wasn't evidence, because I didn't do anything wrong. I absolutely did not hit Tony in the face and knock him out. Not only would I remember that, but he'd been alive and well when I left his shop. Or, more accurately, alive and cranky as ever.

As I flung the back door open, someone pounded on the front door again. "Aly! Open the door! Don't make this harder than it has to be."

Sorry, Charlie, Aly has left the building. You snooze, you lose.

It wouldn't take them long to figure out I'd gone out the back. Doug and Tim were pretty smart, and they didn't have a lot of options. Absent a secret entrance to Narnia in an upstairs, there were only a few places to look for me.

At the edge of our patio, I hung a hard right, veering toward the next-door neighbors who had gone to Florida to visit their kids for Thanksgiving. Instead of the solid fences you'd see in my hometown, back yards in Shady Grove were open. Only a line of thick trees separated our property from the adjacent ones. We'd been back and forth between the houses several times to feed their cat. Between me, Kyle, and the local wildlife, my recent footprints shouldn't stand out among the rest.

Still, I breathed a sigh of relief once the back door clicked shut behind me. Thank goodness no one locked their doors around here. With all the windows and open floor plan, I wasn't comfortable staying in the main living area, or even an upstairs bedroom. What if someone saw my shadow and came to investigate? They should have a basement, though. I'd never needed the basement to feed the cat, but this layout was a mirror image of ours. I found the door easily.

Staying here wasn't a long-term solution, but neither was going back outside. It had been below freezing when I got home, and the temperature would drop dramatically once the sun set.

The neighbor's basement was separated into a big, empty space, a laundry room, and a storage area, just like ours. Unfortunately, no one had left a well-placed disguise or heavy winter coat in the dryer. But I did feel better after moving into the rear storage room and flipping the lock behind me, leaving the lights off. It gave the illusion of security, and for now, that would have to be enough.

The moment I felt reasonably safe, I pulled out my phone to call my brother. Immediately, I realized what a terrible idea that was. He would turn around and come home. Kyle would once again be a sitting duck for Mary.

I couldn't take that risk. The binding spell we'd done at the end of the summer wasn't going to last much longer. She would get her powers back soon. My goal was to make sure she was behind bars before that happened. Preferably with a more permanent binding in place. If Emma and I didn't do the spell to capture Mary this weekend, we might miss our only chance.

Now that I found myself alone and needing aid, sending three magical people out of Shady Grove at once seemed like a terrible idea. But we couldn't have known the police would come looking for me. As soon as I cleared everything up, we could move ahead with the plan.

If only I knew specifically what Sheriff Matthews thought I did, surely I could explain. Maybe I should go back and talk to him and Doug. If I stayed here, they'd find me eventually. Once someone figured out I'd fled through the back door, they would probably go door to door, and everyone in town had heard my neighbors brag about skipping the snow this year. Unfortunately, he was also the type to arrest first, ask questions later. Better to find a safe location, then call.

Ordinarily, the person to save my behind when necessary was my best friend Rusty. He'd happily help me hide bodies if asked. But he was also dating—and now living with—Shady Grove's sole full-time police officer other than the sheriff. Doug was probably currently tearing my house apart looking for evidence. I loved Rusty more than anything, and I'd trust him with my life, but it wasn't fair to test his loyalties.

A chill went down my spine as I wondered if Rusty knew I'd been accused of committing a crime and hadn't told me.

I shook the thought away. My best friend would never let police officers storm my house without giving me a heads up. At a minimum, he'd have facilitated a call where Doug encouraged me to turn myself in. He must have been as clueless as me about the whole thing.

Maybe half an hour had passed since I'd left the bakery. Tony had been cranky but fine when I'd left, so whatever happened must have been very recent. There was no reason for Doug to call his boyfriend on the way to question someone.

There was one other person who would pick me up, no questions asked. Who got a thrill from danger and once stole evidence from the police station for me. If she thought I attacked Tony, Tiffaneigh Pratt would turn me in without blinking. Her dad was, after all, a police officer in Willow Falls. But her sense of adventure and general tendency to challenge authority meant she'd be a good person to help me now.

Without further thought, I pulled out my phone and tapped her name.

"Hey!" She picked up the phone immediately. "I'm glad you called. I know our microbiology mid-term isn't for two weeks but—"

"Stop. Listen closely. Don't say anything to let anyone know who you're talking to, including Brad, if he's there." Our former group project partner and Tiffaneigh's current boyfriend.

She snorted. "Brad Who? I dumped him weeks ago. Which you'd know if you ever went for coffee with me."

"Sorry, I've been busy. Which brings me to why I'm calling."

"Oh, yeah? Need a favor, call Tiff? Is that how this works?"

I winced, but she wasn't wrong. Thankfully, she didn't truly sound upset. But when I spoke, my voice came out small. "I got Tony the Baker's hat in the mail and when I put it on a had a vision and now police are at my house, looking for me."

"At your house? Where are you?"

"Depends. Can you come get me?"

"You know I can."

I thought for a few seconds. The park where Kyle played with his friends was close enough for me to walk while staying in the backyards between here and there. As long as none of my neighbors looked out the window and called the police, I should be safe enough. It was still early for the nine-to-five workers to be home, and this time of year, the sun was already setting. The shadows should protect me.

"I don't want the police to see you driving up. Can you pick me up at the park over on Pheasant and Fifth Street?"

"No problem. Why are they looking for you over a stolen baker's hat?"

"It's not the hat." I swallowed before plunging ahead with the thought I really hadn't wanted to let crystalize in my mind. But there wasn't a lot of room for interpretation in my vision. "I think they think I attacked him."

Tiffaneigh didn't miss a beat. "I'm on my way."

CHAPTER FIVE

THAT WAS what I loved about Tiffaneigh: Take a class together, and she would do everything in her power to obliterate you from the bell curve. Get hit with a magic hat and an assault accusation? She doesn't even ask if you did it before offering help. She was a true friend when it mattered.

I felt much better when I left the basement and eased my way into the neighbors' yard. They had a side door facing away from my house, which helped. Even though I couldn't see what Sheriff Matthews and Doug were up to, it made me feel better to be out of their line of sight.

Every stray bird call and dog bark made me jump about ten feet, but finally, I made it to the park. We didn't have a lot of time. I didn't know if the police would try to follow me when they realized I wasn't in the house, or if they'd leave and look for me somewhere else. Given the number of places in Shady Grove I was likely to turn up—there was here, the coffee shop owned by my brother's girlfriend, the antique store where I worked, and the bowling alley where everyone hung out—it wouldn't take them long to find me. Especially since I didn't bowl.

A lifetime passed before a sedate, dark blue sedan stopped

in front of me. The driver wore huge sunglasses and such an enormous straw hat, it took me a moment to recognize Tiffaneigh. She wasn't driving her trademark fiery red Mustang. Now that I thought about it, it probably wasn't smart to call the person who drove one of the most recognizable cars in Shady Grove. Few people owned vintage cars with a convertible top around here, and no one else had her QNTIFF license plate.

"Your dad's car?" I asked as I slid into the passenger seat. We'd taken it last time we needed to do a little sleuthing together. "Smart thinking."

"I figured you didn't call me because of my looks." She flashed me a smile and shifted the car into gear. "Now hold on and keep your head down."

She pulled away from the curb so fast, I fell backward against the seat. The tires squealed on the pavement.

"Careful," I said when I could breathe normally again. "You don't want to get pulled over."

"Who would pull me over? Both of Shady Grove's officers are busy looking for you." A valid point, so I didn't argue. She tapped the dashboard. "Besides, I've got Dad's scanner. They're headed to Main Street to look for you at Missing Pieces."

Good thing I hadn't gone to Olive for help.

Tiffaneigh turned the radio up, and soon Alicia Keys' voice filled the car. I wondered if "Girl on Fire" was an intentional choice on her part.

For a few minutes, I chewed on my lower lip while trying to figure out what my next step should be. At my direction, my friend kept driving. Eventually, we'd have to figure out where to go, but my brain was having trouble focusing the way I needed it to.

After about ten minutes, Tiffaneigh turned the radio down. "I want you to know that I'm perfectly happy to drive you in circles all day, but did you have a destination in mind?"

Unfortunately, I did not. My initial inclination was to run, but we had a spell to do tomorrow. I couldn't just take off. But I didn't see another immediate option. I could come back once I proved my innocence. "Maybe the train station? I could head down to New York City and hide with Sam until things blow over."

"If police are that interested in finding you, they'll have both train stations and the bus station on alert." She tapped the police scanner again. "And they *are* that interested in finding you."

"Airport?" The nearest one was in Albany, which meant going back through Shady Grove to get to the highway. My next closest option was Montreal. Crossing the border while police were looking for me felt like a bad idea. Especially when I didn't have a passport or even my driver's license on me. I hadn't thought to grab my wallet on the way out of the house. "Never mind. I can't buy a plane ticket without my wallet. What about the bus station? Can I borrow fifty bucks?"

"You still need an ID. I could buy it, but if they check, you won't be allowed to board. Hey, next week, we should go get fake IDs."

She sounded as cheerful and excited as if suggesting we do an escape room.

I groaned. "One crisis at a time, please?"

"Right. Sorry. Listen. Running away isn't the answer. We've got to clear your name," Tiffaneigh said. "How do we prove you didn't hurt Tony?"

More importantly: How did we prove it before tomorrow? We needed to do the spell on the anniversary of Katrina's death. That could not happen if I was either in jail or on the run. I heaved a heavy sigh.

"I'd like to think my word has value, but something tells

me that sitting down with Sheriff Matthews right now would be a big mistake."

"Yeah, I know. Guilty until proven otherwise, as far as the police are concerned. Dad always says that innocence stuff is for the jury. Where were you when you hit Tony?"

I thought back to my vision. "In the bakery, I think. I saw the two of us in a commercial kitchen. He was wearing his chef's coat. But it wasn't real. It can't be."

She ignored my last point. "Did the room look like the kitchen of Let's Bake a Deal?"

"I don't know. I've only ever been in front of the counter, buying stuff."

"Did you see anything else? Mixers, anything cooling on the counters?"

I closed my eyes, trying to recall the unsettling images. "I was holding something…wood, I think. A cylinder with a handle."

She turned her head and looked at me. "Are you talking about a rolling pin? You don't know what a rolling pin is?"

My cheeks grew warm. "Um, maybe? I don't bake much, but now that you mention it…"

"Don't you watch baking shows with Kyle?" Not waiting for an answer, Tiffaneigh put on her turn signal and slowed the car.

"He watches. I mostly do homework."

"You should start paying attention. Rolling pins are common in bakeries."

We went around one turn, then another. From my vantage point cowering on the floor in front of the passenger seat, I had no idea where we might be.

"Hold on," I said. "Where are you taking me?"

"We're going to Let's Bake a Deal. We might find a clue."

The words filled me with dread. Nope. No way. Uh-uh.

"Don't you watch cop shows?" I hissed. "You never return to the scene of the crime."

"We're not returning to the scene, because there was no crime," she replied. "Right?"

"According to my vision, *someone* hit Tony in the face. It just wasn't me. What if someone sees me? It'll be totally suspicious. Or I could leave DNA behind. That always happens on TV."

"We'll make a point not to cut you or spit on the floors. Besides, you haven't touched Tony, have you?"

"Of course not!"

"Then what are you worried about? If your vision showed you attacking Tony and you didn't, maybe there's been a mistake. Let's go look around. Figure out what's going on. If we find Tony, we'll ask him what happened. If necessary, you can handcuff him to yourself and drag him to the police station."

"I don't have handcuffs."

"Use mine." She reached into the console and tossed me a pair. I opened my mouth, then closed it. Some things you didn't want to know.

We must have been on one of the main roads because she hit the accelerator. The car sailed forward. I said, "Listen, I really don't want to go back to the bakery. My visions are never wrong, and I saw someone hitting Tony. I just don't know why it looked like me."

"Maybe going to the bakery will tell us."

With a sigh of resignation, I leaned my cheek against the bottom seat cushion. Cowering in the front seat of a mid-sized sedan was exactly as comfortable as you'd expect.

On the dashboard, the scanner crackled to life. "Suspect spotted at Hyde Park, near the playground."

The response came immediately. I recognized the voice as Sheriff Matthews's. "You sure?"

"Witness says their kids play together sometimes. Definitely knows the suspect, confirms she's familiar with the park," the voice said.

"Any idea where she went?"

"Didn't say, but she's in a dark blue Honda, license plate Tango—."

Tiffaneigh reached over and shut the scanner off. "Uh-oh. They're onto us. We'll have to ditch the car."

"Great. Let me just grab something out of my spare garage," I said. Being accused of a crime and then having to cower beneath the dashboard of a car was making me cranky. "Can I at least sit up now that they know I'm with you?"

"I guess. They don't know where we are."

"Are you sure about that?" I gestured toward the scanner. "You shut it off."

"Touché." Tiffaneigh reached to turn the device back on, but before she got there, a siren made her hand jerk back. "Um, don't panic."

"Too late."

She slammed on the accelerator and the car lurched forward. "It's okay. He was passing us in the other direction and had to make a three-point turn. Skidded into a snowbank. That should buy us a little time."

I shot her a genuine smile. "Thanks. I know you didn't sign up for this when Professor Zimm made us lab partners."

"Are you kidding? This is the most fun I've had in ages. I wish all my friends were like you."

She yanked the wheel, squealing around the corner and sending my lunch shooting up into the back of my throat. A bacon cheeseburger definitely tasted better the first time around. Unable to reply, I gripped the armrest on my door for dear life.

Behind us, the police car also turned. Tiffaneigh whipped the wheel once, then again. It took me a minute to realize she was still heading for the bakery.

"Shouldn't we go somewhere else?"

"Don't be silly. We've got a solid plan." Tiffaneigh slammed on the brakes. "Now get out."

I gaped at her. "Are you high?"

She hit the unlock button and leaned across me to open the passenger door. "They can't see us. You've got about thirty seconds to hide before they come around the corner. They should keep following me."

A wave of gratitude washed over me. There was no time to thank her, but tears welled in my eyes as I jumped out of the car and slammed the door.

Tiffaneigh's voice carried through the sunroof as she peeled away from the curb. "You're welcome!"

The sound of police sirens grew closer, and I raced for an open dumpster. Good thing I'd been taking self-defense classes. A year ago, I wouldn't have been in good enough shape to manage this. Grabbing the top, I leapt and pulled as hard as I could. There was no time to be graceful, so I went head first and wrapped my arms over my head to break my fall. A cloud of flour billowed around me as I landed on a giant bag. I fought not to cough.

My eyes streamed with tears. It felt like eons later, but was probably about ten seconds, when the police sirens continued past the dumpster. Using them for cover, I coughed frantically and waved the flour out of my nose. The sirens continued to move away from me, so I went to the back door of the bakery and twisted the knob.

Locked.

Wonderful. Now what?

There was a small window on the wall, a couple of feet above the dumpster. It appeared to be open, although a screen kept bugs out. The screen could be removed for me to get in, but would I fit? The entire window frame was about six inches high. My head had to be bigger than that. But since I couldn't measure it, I'd need to climb up and try to wiggle inside.

A sound tore through the air: tires skidding, a crash. A wail of anguish. A *female* wail.

"Tiffaneigh!"

Her name tore from me without thinking. Then, as abruptly as the screaming started, it cut off. My heart stopped.

No.

She had to be okay.

More brakes squealing. I listened as hard as I could, but I needed to get closer. There was no way I could enter that bakery without making sure Tiffaneigh was safe first. Not after everything she did for me.

Taking a deep breath, I rose to my feet, not even bothering to brush the flour off myself. Keeping close to the wall of the alley, I crept toward the corner where Tiffaneigh had vanished. The sirens stopped, but flashing blue and red lights bounced off the bricks at the front of the alleyway. When I got to the end, I peered around the corner, terrified of what I would see.

There, a couple of blocks down. Moving red and blue lights illuminated Mr. Pratt's car where it lay flipped upside down on the pavement. Two police cars were parked beside it, and a man stood beside the car, looking inside. Probably Doug, from the size of him, but it was hard to tell from this distance.

As I stood there, wondering what on earth to do next, an ambulance pulled silently onto the scene. No sirens. No flashing lights.

My stomach dropped out of me. No sirens and no lights meant no urgency. No urgency meant she was dead.

Gone.

I'd killed my friend.

A scream of agony escaped me as I fell to my knees. When the officers at the scene turned to look, I didn't even care. Before they got close enough to make out their faces, I passed out.

CHAPTER SIX

THE PACKAGE LOOKED COMPLETELY NORMAL. U.S. Priority Mail medium-sized box, just like my mom used whenever mailing us gifts.

Whoa. I shook my head, blinking rapidly.

Why did I feel like I'd done this before?

The rest of the mail went straight into the recycling bin left by the front door for that purpose: bills for my brother, *Highlights Kids* for Kyle. Wait. I fished that one out and set it on the entry table. Then I turned the box over in my hands to examine it.

My name was on the label, like I knew it would be. But how?

And just like that, everything came rushing back. Police, Tony, hiding, calling Tiffaneigh for help, going to the bakery.

The package dropped onto my feet, but I barely felt the impact. What was happening? A few seconds ago, I watched my friend die in a car crash because police officers were after me. Unless I'd been daydreaming too much while collecting the mail.

No, that didn't make sense. What was going on?

Maybe the package had sent me the strongest and most realistic vision ever. Wow! Scary.

That had to be the answer. Even though my visions had always been of the past, maybe something had shifted. I needed to call Olive.

Shaking my head, I blinked a few times to get the horrible sights and sounds out of my mind. My hands shook when I bent to retrieve the package and put it on the table.

Before I did anything else, I needed to make sure Tiffaneigh was okay. That my horrible vision hadn't happened because I was experiencing her death real-time through someone else's eyes. When I pulled out my phone, the screen came to life, flashing the time. Two-fifty-seven p.m. Weird. I'd thought that was what it said earlier.

She answered on the first ring. "Hey. I'm glad you called. I know our microbiology mid-term isn't for two weeks but we should really set up our study schedule now. What nights are you at work?"

Exactly the way she greeted me in my vision. That could not be a good sign. Instead of interrupting her like before, it took me almost fifteen seconds to shake off the feeling of dread settling over me enough to speak.

"Yeah, let's do that. Olive will give me any evenings I need off to study, but this semester I usually work Tuesday, Thursday, and Sunday. Listen, this is going to sound weird but... Are you okay?"

"Sure, I guess. Still a little annoyed that Brad turned me into a basketball widow, but I'll get over it. Already there, actually."

Wait. That sounded familiar. "You and Brad broke up?"

"Yeah, we did. You would know that if you ever met me for coffee."

How could I have possibly known that? Sure, she'd mentioned it in the vision I'd just had, but again—my visions were supposed to be of past events. Tiffaneigh telling me she broke up with Brad wasn't the kind of thing momentous enough to leave visions on my phone. Or to leave visions in the package sitting on the floor where I'd left it.

Something was wrong.

My mind flew in a thousand directions at once. This was too real to be a dream, too lengthy to be a vision. Plus, in my visions, I couldn't control things I said or did. Never once did I choose to make a phone call. I was in the past moment, living out someone else's experiences. Everything had already happened, so I'd never been able to make any changes. I existed in my visions as a passenger, solely along for the ride.

Not what had happened when I found the baker's hat. Not at all.

"Aly? Are you still there?"

"Yeah, sorry." I promised Tiffaneigh that we'd hang out to study soon, then hung up. I needed to figure out what was going on.

Olive would know. Whenever anything went wrong with my powers, she was the one who helped. And this was a doozy of a problem. I pulled my phone out again.

Someone pounded on the door. I jumped. My phone clattered to the floor and skittered under the table. A deep, familiar voice boomed through the wood. "Aluminum Reynolds! This is the police. Come out with your hands up!"

Oh, fluorine.

CHAPTER SEVEN

SOMEHOW, I'd traveled back in time. But why? How? And also, why? But how? Those thoughts had barely finished flitting through my head when, for the second time in less than two hours, I turned and bolted through my house, out the back door.

I had already locked myself in the neighbor's basement before realizing I'd left my phone where it landed in the front hall. No way to call for help, although I definitely couldn't reach out to Tiffaneigh again. Not after seeing what happened. Most people never got a second chance to save the people they loved, and I wasn't going to throw mine away.

The police would find my phone when they broke the door down, and they'd probably figure out I'd been home when they knocked. Also, I assumed the package sitting on the floor still contained Tony's baker's hat, unless I'd hallucinated everything. But watching everything else repeat seemed too real for that. I'd never known anyone to have a spot-on hallucination of the future; my visions only worked looking back.

Note to self: If you go back in time again, grab the package on your way out the door. Don't drop your phone. Also, figure out how you went back in time.

I couldn't stay here. Doug would see my phone, know I never left the house without it, and come find me as soon as they discovered I wasn't in my room. If I were very lucky, they'd think I dropped it on my way out the front door and went down the shoveled path, but—today didn't exactly feel like my lucky day. They'd find my car in the garage soon enough and know I wouldn't have gotten far on foot. Former California girls did not go for snowy strolls in early December.

Last time this happened, a concerned citizen spotted me getting into Tiffaneigh's car. It was probably a fluke. This time, I would be more careful. Maybe I could find a bicycle somewhere. Or escape on foot. I could stick to the shadows, hide somewhere no one would think to look for me.

Unfortunately, that ruled out going to Olive for help. While listening to the scanner, Tiffaneigh had told me that Missing Pieces was Sheriff Matthews's first stop once he discovered I wasn't home. He'd probably go himself while sending Doug to check Kevin's office, which ruled out my second hiding place. The Patels lived uncomfortably close to my house. Where else could I go?

Julie? Kevin's girlfriend would probably be willing to help, and as a former lawyer herself, she wouldn't leave me to talk to the police on my own. She might try to convince me to turn myself in, but at least she'd stick with me.

The problem was, her coffee shop, On What Grounds?, shared an alley with Missing Pieces. Even if the sheriff's department didn't think to look for me at the place where I got caffeine almost daily, which was unlikely, the odds of someone spotting me going in were too high.

Emma. The friend I'd made during last summer's Shady Grove Annual Treasure Hunt had turned out to be a powerful ally—and an equally strong witch. She'd helped reverse

Mary's spell that stole my powers last summer, and she was planning to anchor me tomorrow. Maybe she could help now?

If she couldn't, her magical cat always had something useful to say. Emma would welcome me and protect me, but she lived miles away in Willow Falls. With my car back at my house, it would be a long walk in subzero temperatures once the sun set.

At least it would be harder for anyone to see me—the route didn't have any street lights. No other obvious options jumped out. I still didn't want to involve Rusty. It might take weeks to get to Emma's place, but she ran a home for lost souls. If ever a soul felt lost, it was this one. At the moment, she appeared to be my best option. I better get started.

Five minutes later, I was calling myself ten kinds of names while still trudging down the street, jumping every time a car went by. This would never work. There had to be a better way to figure out what was going on. Until I thought of one, however, I kept walking.

Note to Self, #2: if you go back in time again, grab the darn baker's hat *and* a jacket. And maybe my car keys. Hmmm. I'd wasted time initially examining the baker's hat and having that vision. I'd lost time today trying to figure out what happened and calling Tiffaneigh. What if I'd taken the package and raced straight for the garage? Maybe I would have made it to my car?

Oh, well. It was too late to worry about that now. Or possibly too early.

After another five minutes, curses started tumbling out of my mouth. This had to be the worst plan I possibly could have come up with. The road from my house to Emma's went directly through Shady Grove. Driving around town instead of through it wouldn't take much time, but I was on foot. It would take at least another hour of walking around if I stayed on the side streets and residential areas.

Someone was going to see me. I needed to get off the streets, pronto.

Missing Pieces sat near the middle of Main Street. From two blocks down, I easily spotted the police car sitting out front. They weren't even trying to hide their presence. Until they left, that was out. The magic shop was on the other side of Missing Pieces. Although Amira would help, I didn't see an obvious way to get to her from my current position. But on this end of the street, I stood outside a shop that sold maternity clothes. Only five feet further down the sidewalk sat the pet store. A pet store where I was very familiar with the owner.

Yes! Jeff Ahn would help me. He'd said he owed me one.

Keeping my head low, I darted into Paws and Effect and shut the front door behind me. A few customers wandered around, but none of them seemed to notice me. Jeff stood behind the cash register. I made a beeline for him. As soon as I got behind the relative safety of the counter, I dropped to the ground.

"This is a nice surprise," Jeff said. "How are you?"

"Act natural," I said. "Pretend I'm not here."

"You're sitting on my foot."

"Oops." I shifted my weight.

A customer approached, so I waited patiently while Jeff made small talk and rang up their purchases. Then another had a question about the cats. Nearly ten minutes passed before the bolt on the front door clacked into place. Then Jeff squatted down beside me.

"Can I help you?" he asked.

"Is everyone gone?"

"Yeah. We're closed."

"Good. I need your help."

Quickly I explained everything that had happened to me since arriving home to find an unmarked package on my front porch.

"You're psychic, right?" Jeff said. "Shouldn't your powers have told you not to touch that?"

"I wish. But it doesn't matter. Even if I hadn't picked it up, the police are after me." I paused. "I think I know why. If my vision is accurate, someone attacked Tony. Sheriff Matthews saw me leaving the bakery. Tony was fine when I left, though. What happened in those few minutes? How did the hat get to me? It's not like Sheriff Matthews could have gotten a psychic reading and then sent it on over via messenger pigeon."

"Are you sure about that? What if he asked someone else?"

I didn't want to pretend no one else in Shady Grove had any magical powers. Not when Jeff owed me a favor because I helped him after one of his spells had a very unfortunate, unforeseen consequence. But even if someone else had my specific gifts, I didn't see Sheriff Matthews consulting them for help with a murder case. Or letting the key evidence go to the prime suspect if he had. I said so.

"A fair point," Jeff conceded.

"Also, there wasn't time," I said. "When I left the bakery, Sheriff Matthews was outside talking to his girlfriend. He was at my house roughly half an hour later. He must have finished talking to her, gone inside and seen whatever he saw. Someone had to go in the back door, attack Tony, and leave within a very short time frame."

"How can I help?" Jeff asked.

"I'm hoping you'll go with me to the bakery. I need you to climb through the open window. Go in, look around, and find any evidence of magic or anything that happened. Then tell me what you found. Also, maybe bring me a cupcake? Tony refused to sell them to me earlier, and it's been a two-cupcake day, at least."

Jeff studied me thoughtfully. "Let me get this straight. You want me to shift into bunny shape, enter the bakery, and steal evidence from the crime scene?"

"You make that sound like a bad thing. Besides, the cupcakes shouldn't be evidence."

"Just wanted to make sure we're clear." His tone betrayed his amusement. "Now I understand why you're asking me for help instead of Olive. I suppose I do owe you a favor, although to be honest, I didn't think this would be the type of thing you'd ask."

"I'm sorry. I wouldn't ask if it wasn't extremely important."

"I know." Jeff glanced out the front window. "We can't walk down Main Street together. The police car is in front of Missing Pieces. Tell you what. I'll walk over, go inside, see what I can find out, and report back."

"What do I do?"

"Rest? List your enemies. Think of people who disliked Tony. Try to figure out who would hurt him and frame you. Also people who could curse a hat. The options are nearly limitless." Jeff started to go, then stopped and turned back. "When was the last time you ate?"

I thought for a minute. "In actual time, since lunch. About four hours ago. In Bizarro Time Blip World? I don't know, maybe six or seven?"

"Too long. I'll pick you up a sandwich and coffee at On What Grounds? on the way back."

At his words, my stomach rumbled. I hadn't even realized how hungry I was until he asked. "Thanks, Jeff. You're a lifesaver."

The overhead lights went out. A moment later, the rear door slammed shut, leaving me alone with my thoughts. My thoughts were not pleasant. I didn't want to be alone with them.

At least if I had my phone, I could do some research. Not that research would be super useful when I didn't know what to look up. Fake visions? Time travel? How to avoid future events coming true? Who would frame Aly Reynolds for murder?

The day's events had worn me out more than I thought. My brain felt like mush. Thinking beyond the sustenance Jeff promised me felt impossible. Soon enough, my eyelids grew heavy. I tilted my head back, expecting to rest just for a minute. Jeff wouldn't be gone long. Plenty of time to research while I ate.

The moment my lashes touched my cheeks, I drifted off to sleep.

CHAPTER EIGHT

I JERKED AWAKE WITH A START.

My head banged against a shelf under the counter. Ow. What the—where was I? Oh, right. The pet store. Jeff had promised to go check out the bakery and come back.

How long had he been gone? I scrambled for my phone, suddenly worried that while I'd been napping, he'd been caught by the police and hauled off to jail for breaking into a crime scene. While in bunny form. Then I remembered I'd left it at home.

A clock above the register displayed the time in large red letters. 9:08 pm. No way. That was impossible. Sure, I'd been tired, but how could I have slept for hours? It didn't take that long to walk here from my house, did it? Although I wasn't sure exactly when he left, Jeff should have been back a while ago.

A tapping at the front door made the hair on the back of my neck stand up. One, two, three, then again. The pattern repeated. That must be what had woken me. Who was trying to get in? Jeff had a key.

The front blinds were down but not entirely shut. Someone standing outside the door might see enough to tell that someone was inside, even with the lights off. Keeping low to the floor, I crept over, trying desperately to get a view without whoever was outside seeing my face.

To my surprise, a gray and white bunny stood on the doormat outside, shivering. His nose twitched furiously. If a bunny could look exhausted, this one did. While I watched, he tapped again. Then our eyes met. The bunny hopped in place.

This couldn't be good.

Scrambling to my feet, I twisted the deadbolt and cracked the door just enough for the poor creature to sneak in. Then I hurriedly shut the door, closed the blinds the rest of the way, and sank to the floor.

"You know, I expected you to shift into human form when you left the bakery. It must have taken you ages to hop down Main Street."

Not to mention, rabbits couldn't carry sandwiches and coffee.

I waited for him to shift back into human form. Nothing happened.

"Jeff? Are you okay?"

The rabbit shook his head.

"Did something happen at the bakery?"

If a rabbit could shrug, that was the best way to describe this particular gesture. My spine tingled.

"Okay, this isn't funny anymore. Turn into Jeff and tell me what you saw. I need to find the killer in the next few hours. I've got big plans for tomorrow."

The rabbit hopped over to the counter, stood on his hind legs, and stretched for the top. Then he looked back at me. To the register, to me. Again. A third time. What was happening?

"You want up? No problem." Gently, I picked Jeff up and set him on the surface. "Don't blame me if this thing cracks under your human weight, though."

I kept the words light, but this turn of events made me

extremely nervous. When I first met Jeff, Shady Grove experienced a magical earthquake that inadvertently trapped him in bunny form. It took the help of two experienced witches plus a magical orb to undo the spell. None of which I happened to have with me at the moment.

Bending down, I looked Jeff in the eye. "I need you to promise this isn't a joke. Are you okay?"

The rabbit moved his head left to right, left to right. *No.*

"This is Jeff, right? I'm not dreaming?"

He moved his head up and down, up and down. *Yes.*

"Can you shift back and talk to me?"

He shook his head again.

"Are you stuck?"

Another nod.

Oh, no. For the second time in a few short months, poor Jeff couldn't shift out of bunny form. And once again, it was all my fault.

No. I wouldn't let this happen. Wouldn't let him stay like this. If Sheriff Matthews wasn't still at Missing Pieces waiting for me to show up, he'd be at the police station. It wasn't far.

Gently, I gave Jeff a hug. "I'm so sorry. I will fix this, but first, I have to know what happened. Is that okay?"

Another nod.

Using the head shake and nod format was tedious.

"Wait here," I told Jeff. "I have an idea."

If rabbits could talk, this one absolutely would have said, "Where do you think I'm going to go?"

The first time I'd been to Paws and Effect, there had been a storage room in the back. For the most part, it housed things like bags of dog food. But there were also some empty cardboard boxes, broken down and waiting to be taken out to the dumpster. After asking Jeff to lead me to a box cutter, I sliced a box open and laid it out on the ground. Jeff showed me where to get markers, and I created a giant alphabet on the blank side of the cardboard.

"Here. You step on the letters, okay?" I drew an empty square at the bottom. "Between words, come here to tell me to make a space. I'll write down what you tell me."

The rabbit nodded.

"Sorry we don't have a better way to communicate." Then I drew two big circles, with "yes" inside one and "no" inside the other. Then I set the marker down, grabbed a pad of paper and a pen, and settled cross-legged onto the floor beside the box.

It felt like hours passed before Jeff conveyed any useful information using this mechanic, but it was all we had. Eventually I learned that the store was closed and locked. Then Jeff spelled out "T-A-P-E".

"Tape? There was crime scene tape at the scene?"

He hopped to the Yes circle and looked at me.

"I suppose that makes sense. Did you see a chalk outline of a body, like on TV?"

Yes.

That stopped me for a second. Even though I'd had the vision, and even though police showed up at my house—twice—I hadn't really believed anything serious happened to Tony. Mostly because I knew with one hundred percent certainty that he was uninjured when I left the bakery. I couldn't think what would have changed before Sheriff Matthews entered a few minutes later.

But now, to think, he might actually be dead. My stomach sank.

The answer to my next question seemed obvious, but I asked it anyway. "Was it the right size to be Tony?"

Yes.

Not sure it would have helped me if he'd said no, but too late to worry about that now.

"You didn't see his baker's hat, did you?"

Maybe the one sent to me was a spare or a fake or something. I didn't know. I was grasping at straws, trying to have a conversation with a rabbit who spelled out words with his feet.

No.

I slumped to the ground, exhausted. What did all this mean? Also, why was Jeff stuck as a bunny? To date, there was only one person we knew who had the ability to cast a spell that might override his magic.

…A person who also probably had the power to attach a false vision to a baker's hat.

…Or to make herself look like me.

…And had a reason to distract me while she went after my nephew. Whether she knew he was out of town or not, putting me out of commission would only help whatever nefarious plans Mary had in mind. She must have killed Tony to get the police to arrest me.

A shudder went down my spine. Her powers had come back.

We were too late. We should have done the spell earlier.

My eyes filled with tears, and I sank to the ground. My head dropped into my hands. We'd thought waiting until the anniversary of the day Katrina died would give us a boost when using the orb to catch her killer. But apparently, all we'd done was make Mary mad.

I didn't have the first clue how to explain to Sheriff Matthews that I wasn't the murderer, it was actually a witch with a vendetta against me. He'd think I was setting myself up for an insanity plea.

On top of that, I'd somehow gotten Jeff trapped in bunny form. Again. Poor Jeff.

Poor *Tony.* He might be a jerk, but he didn't deserve to die.

Jeff hopped into my lap, nuzzling my arm. I stroked his head. "I'm so sorry about this. I swear, I had no idea what would happen. But I'll figure this out. We did it once, we can do it again."

Hmmm. If I could figure out how to travel back in time

again, would Jeff automatically revert to his human form? How would I do that? Earlier, Tiffaneigh died. I wasn't going to kill Jeff. I kept sitting there, stroking my friend's soft bunny head, too bone-tired to move.

The only sound was the ticking clock. Time was so funny. Marching endlessly forward, even when you wished it wouldn't. Until you got stuck reliving the same day over and over....

It was all too much. Closing my eyes, I tried to block out the sound. But I quickly realized that I was so tired, a marching band could have come through the store and I wouldn't have noticed.

Shifting my position, I laid down on the floor, and Jeff snuggled up against my side. Not the least comfortable I'd been today. Then I closed my eyes and waited for sleep to claim me.

CHAPTER NINE

THE THIRD TIME I found myself in my front entryway holding that stupid package, everything fell into place. I hadn't mysteriously traveled into the past by accident. I hadn't done it myself through some previously undiscovered but very welcome superpower. Nope. I was caught in a time loop. I should've seen it sooner.

With a sound of disgust, I let the rest of the mail fall to the ground. What was the point of sorting and recycling it? Sheriff Matthews and Doug were on their way to arrest me. I needed to go, pronto. No reason to waste precious seconds.

Before leaving, I patted my pocket to secure my phone. No leaving it behind if I could help it. Then I raced out the front door, straight for the neighbor's house.

…Right across the front and side lawns.

The snow-covered front and side lawns. Which now showed a perfect line of footprints. Also, my feet were wet.

Oh, fluorine. This would never work. I couldn't go inside now. I might as well have drawn them a map. Before, I'd moved across our wooden deck, through the brush, onto the Hendersons' concrete patio. Now, even the worst detective in the state could plainly see that someone had stood on our front porch and run to the neighbor's house.

Maybe they'd think it was the UPS guy or a meter reader, but I doubted it. Ugh.

Sirens in the distance told me that unless getting arrested was part of the universe's plan for me, my time in this loop was limited. It wasn't even worth trying to keep running. Maybe if they took me away, I'd learn something interesting from the interrogation. Since I was going to get caught, I should use the conversation to my advantage.

It was freezing out here, so I let myself into the Hendersons' living room and plopped down on their couch. While I waited for Sheriff Matthews and Doug to arrive, I texted Jeff. *Are you stuck in bunny form? If so, please step on the Y and then hop to ENTER.*

Seconds later, my phone beeped. *Have you been sniffing too many chemicals in the science lab?* Directly below it, Jeff had sent a selfie where he wore an exaggeratedly concerned expression.

My whole body relaxed. I hadn't realized just how worried this made me until finding out he was okay. I texted back, *Will explain later. Please stay human, just in case.*

He sent me a thumbs up.

Thank goodness for small favors. Now I didn't have to worry about Jeff until this got resolved.

My driveway remained clear of police cars, so I removed the hat from its package. This time, I examined the box a little more closely. The same USPS Priority Mail packaging I'd noticed earlier. Same smeary lettering that clearly did *not* resemble my mother's under scrutiny. Not to mention, a much lighter box than anything Mom ever sent. Her care packages were crammed full of anything she could think to stuff in there. I should've been suspicious from the start. And again, this hadn't been mailed.

The police would be here soon. All I needed to do was

show them the box. They had fancy crime labs. It wouldn't make any sense for me to have brought it home, put it in a package addressed to myself, and pretend to have gotten it in the mail—yet not even bothered to put a stamp on it, much less a postmark. Doug knew me better than that. They'd have to believe that, whatever was going on, this was all a big mistake.

Back to my scrutiny. Who put the hat on my doorstep? And why?

I turned the package over and over in my hands. It looked exactly the way it had earlier, and I still didn't know how it appeared on my doorstep. But now I'd probably managed to obliterate any fingerprints with my careless handling. Argh!

The thought that Mary might have been leaving a package on my porch and ringing the bell while I stood not fifty feet away inside the kitchen made me want to kick myself. What kind of detective was I? My arch nemesis just strolled on up to my front door, and I didn't even notice.

To make myself feel better, I decided she could have used a third party to make the delivery. Hopefully, she tipped them well for ruining my day.

Okay, Aly. Focus. The hat had given me a vision earlier. Could I get one from the box itself? How did one use a package? Should I take it to the mailbox and put it inside?

The sirens outside grew louder. That was a negative on walking to the mailbox. Closing my eyes, I imagined handing the box to the extremely friendly Black man who worked at the post office. I heard him saying, "Good morning" to Kyle in his big, booming voice. I held the box out as if he really stood in front of me.

Nothing happened.

In the distance, two car doors slammed. For the third time, I heard Sheriff Matthews yelling at me to open the door. For the third time, I ignored him. They'd find me soon enough. No need to make their job easier than I'd already done. Meanwhile, we had a video doorbell. My brother could check his phone and tell me who'd left the package.

Now that I thought about it, I was surprised he hadn't texted me yet. Usually he'd let me know to bring stuff inside before it got destroyed by the weather. In New York, a couple of hours could mean at least three thunderstorms or massive temperature drops. You never knew what could happen to cardboard left outside.

Pulling out my phone, I called Kevin. It went to voice mail. "Big brother, call me back. I need help."

"Aluminum Reynolds! There you are. Don't move. Put your hands in the air."

The voice bellowed through the now-open front door, bouncing off the walls. I hadn't bothered to lock it behind me. What was the point? Still, hearing my name made me jump. My phone clattered to the hardwood floor and skidded over to the far wall. Wonderful. I should tie the thing to my wrist next time.

"No sudden moves. Put your hands on your head."

Following the voice's instructions, I turned around slowly. Not surprisingly, Sheriff Matthews aimed his gun at me.

Score one for the Shady Grove police department. They'd found me as easily as expected.

"Drop it!"

My phone? I'd already—oh. The package. I'd forgotten I still clutched the box in one hand. Bending my knees slowly, I set it on the ground. Sure, it (most likely) only contained a hat, but one that must have been infused with some kind of spell. I didn't want to know what dropping a cursed hat might do.

"Now push it toward me," he said. "That's a good girl."

I'd been happy to comply until those last two words. "There's no need to be condescending."

"I'm fairly certain you're not in a position to tell me how to behave, *Ms. Reynolds*." He moved toward me. "It really was bad luck that I happened to be walking by when you left the bakery. Bad for you, I mean. Probably the easiest crime I ever solved."

"I don't know what you're talking about," I said. "Tony was fine when I left."

"Then how do you know this is about Tony? No one said his name. I haven't mentioned Tony. Doug hasn't mentioned Tony."

Because I had a vision of Tony getting smacked in the face with a rolling pin, I didn't tell him. Instead, I went with the obvious answer. "You just mentioned running into me outside the bakery. I drew a logical conclusion."

"Right. Outside Let's Bake a Deal. Where you lied and said you forgot your wallet. But I know that's not true, because I found a receipt on the ground inside. A whole lot of purchases at I'll Put a Spell on You. Amira was happy to confirm that you made them just a few minutes before we ran into each other."

Under ordinary circumstances, I might be disappointed in my friend for selling me out, but she couldn't have known why they were asking.

"Buying magical supplies isn't a crime," I pointed out. "Neither is lying about not having any money. Or dropping a receipt. You want to fine me for littering? Go ahead."

"True. But you know what is a crime? Murder."

Murder. He'd said it. The word punched me in the gut. They really thought I'd killed someone. How was that even possible? All of a sudden, I could hardly breathe. Even seeing Tony pass out in my vision with my own face above him, even hearing Jeff tell me about a chalk outline, I'd never wanted to believe he was dead.

The idea of me being the one who killed him was absolutely unthinkable. To everyone except the sheriff, apparently. I needed to find out what he knew. This had to be a mistake. A very unfortunate, probably supernatural mistake.

When I spoke, my voice shook. "What happened to Tony?"

"You know the answer to that, Ms. Reynolds, don't you? I think we've chatted long enough. It's time for you to come with me down to the station."

"To be honest, Sheriff, I don't think I want to do that," I said.

"Too bad. Aluminum Reynolds, you're under arrest for the murder of Tony Santoro. You have a right to remain silent."

He stepped forward and pulled a pair of handcuffs from his pocket. Although part of me desperately wanted to run, I didn't want to know whether he would shoot me. Besides, Doug was outside somewhere.

Not knowing what else to do, I held my hands over my head until Sheriff Matthews took my left wrist and clicked a handcuff around it. I shivered when the cold metal touched my flesh. Then he took my other wrist and—

Mercifully, a gray mist descended.

CHAPTER TEN

OH, goody! I stood in Kevin's foyer, holding the package. My phone rested in my pocket where it belonged. I wasn't wearing handcuffs anymore. Sometimes, it really was the little things that made all the difference.

Apparently, getting arrested knocked me to the beginning of this loop, or whatever it was. Since I didn't have any interest in spending time in a jail cell, that was completely okay with me. Not as okay as figuring out what was happening and getting back to my regular life, but I wasn't in a position to be choosy.

From my last loop, I'd confirmed a few important things: first, there wasn't much time between when I found the package and when the police arrived, but there might be enough to get away. Second, someone killed Tony after I left the bakery. Third, the police thought it was me. I didn't blame them. The evidence was compelling.

They weren't going to get a chance to arrest me again, though. I raced for my car, slamming the button to open the garage door on my way past. I dove into the front seat of my Prius, stabbed the ignition button, and shifted into gear in one solid movement. The garage door was still rumbling upward when the car sprang to life. I stomped the accelerator and my car jumped backward, screeching down the driveway.

Left. The police arrived from the left. I reversed in a half circle, pointed my car right, and took off again.

This was a pretty long street, so they'd see me as soon as they rounded the corner. At the first intersection, I swung a left, barely lifting my foot from the accelerator. In my rearview mirror, I hadn't spotted any flashing lights yet, but they couldn't be more than a few seconds away.

Someone screamed.

Instinctively, I stomped on the brakes as I turned to look. My tires skidded on the ice.

Mrs. Chang's cat crouched, frozen, in the middle of the street.

Uh-oh. I yanked at the wheel, desperate to avoid it. The car swerved to the right. So did the cat. I pulled the e-brake. I closed my eyes. I prayed. Mrs. Chang screamed again.

Oh, f—-

CHAPTER ELEVEN

THE PACKAGE LOOKED COMPLETELY NORMAL. U.S. Priority Mail medium-sized box, just like my mom used whenever mailing us gifts.

That was a relief. Note to self: keep your eyes on the road. There was one problem, though: I was too shaken to get back in my car. Even knowing the cat was fine, I could hardly breathe. My knees gave out, and I sank to the stoop. Obviously, I needed to get moving, but my brain barely functioned.

Element one was… Something. Probably a gas. Or a solid.

Deep breaths. Inhale, exhale. I could do this.

At least I knew that if I accidentally ran over an animal, the universe would pop me back here to save its life. A small kindness in this bizarre day.

Pulling out my phone, I tapped Doug's name in my Contacts app.

"Aly?" I should have known he would be surprised to hear from me. He didn't know what I'd been through.

I didn't give him a chance to say more. "You guys suck! I didn't kill Tony, I didn't kill anyone, yet no matter what I do, you just keep showing up at my house, all ready to arrest me.

Why aren't you out there looking for the real killer? I know why! Because your uncle is as crooked as the day is long, and—"

The sight of a police car turning onto my street cut me off. I'd been so wrapped up in my righteous fury, I hadn't even heard the sirens.

Eff it. I might as well try to see if mailing the package would give me a vision. I strolled down the driveway as they approached, refusing to look at the cars.

"If you're done now, I'm supposed to tell you that you have the right to remain silent." He paused. "You know I don't want to do this. But Uncle Tim called in a warrant, and Judge Schaffer gave it to him no problem."

"I was in the wrong place at the wrong time. That's all this is." Closing my eyes, I opened the mailbox and put the package inside. Then I lifted the shut the door, lifted the red flag, and waited.

Nothing happened. This box wasn't going to tell me anything.

I was about to take it out of the mailbox and stomp on it when Doug spoke. "I want to believe you, Aly, I do. You're not a killer. But there wasn't much time between when you left the shop and Uncle walked in. The only exit was locked and bolted from the inside. Unless someone invisible killed Tony and left before Uncle and I searched the place, it doesn't look good. We have to follow the evidence."

A car screeched to a stop in front of me, half in the driveway and half in the street. I jumped backward. Sheriff Matthews was at the wheel. I ignored him.

"Someone set me up." Was this a good time to tell him magic was real, and I was psychic? Would the time loop reset if he wasn't supposed to know? Maybe Amira's ghost killed Tony... said the scientist. Wow, how my life had changed.

Doug's response interrupted my thoughts. "Rusty will

prove it. You know he will. But we have to take you in for questioning."

Ignoring him, I dropped my phone and moved around the police car before Sheriff Matthews exited the vehicle. Cupping my hands over my mouth, I screamed through his driver's side window. "You and the Mayor are ruining Shady Grove! I'm going to run against you myself next time to make sure stuff like this doesn't happen! And I'll win. See if I don't."

Sheriff Matthews rolled down his window, eying me curiously. "Are you done?"

To my right, Doug was slowly walking up the driveway. The handcuffs on his belt glinted ominously in the sunlight. At least his gun was holstered.

"No." Leaning forward, I jabbed the sheriff in the nose as hard as I could. "Now I'm done. You proton."

CHAPTER TWELVE

PRESTO! Abracadabra or whatever. I was back in Kevin's foyer. Woo-hoo!

The package looked completely normal. U.S. Priority Mail medium-sized box, just like my mom used whenever mailing us gifts. Not Mom's handwriting, though. Duh.

Maybe Amira could run some tests on it. Too bad I'll Put a Spell on You was on Main Street. Someone might see my car and head over. But Kevin had his office on Second Street. Maybe I could park in his lot and slink through the back alleys. As long as the lot had been plowed this morning, that might work.

Getting to my car didn't take long. This time, I turned right at the corner, moving away from the cat. While driving, I reviewed the known facts in my mind. There had to be a logical explanation for all of this—even if that logical explanation involved magic. I needed a hypothesis. My first thought was that to get out of this loop, I needed to figure out who killed Tony. At the moment, all I knew was it wasn't me.

Could someone have wiped my memory? Doug said there wasn't time for anyone else to have entered the bakery between when I left and Sheriff Matthews entered. What I didn't know was if Sheriff Matthews had been in sight of the door the entire time he was on the phone. If so, the only other likely suspect was the Sheriff of Shady Grove. Either he did it, or he was covering for someone who did.

But since our local law enforcement didn't have any magical powers that I was aware of, that didn't explain the time loop. If the sheriff or one of his friends killed Tony and framed me, how would magic come into the equation?

My gut told me Mary was behind this day. She certainly had the power. But if she could somehow control me to make me kill Tony—and I wasn't sure that was possible—wouldn't she want me to remember it? Surely I'd be more tortured by having actually killed someone than being falsely arrested. Could she have slipped into the bakery without anyone seeing her, killed Tony, slipped out, and dropped his hat at my house?

Maybe I should skip the magic shop and head for campus instead. We had a science lab where I could dust the box for fingerprints, run the hat to confirm Tony's DNA, and look for any traces of Mary.

This day seemed one hundred percent like a magical creation, though. Time didn't normally repeat itself endlessly. For once, I needed a witch before examining the science.

By the time I turned onto Second Street, I felt a little better. Yelling at the sheriff and poking him in the nose had improved my spirits. Sure, time kept repeating, but I could say or do anything I wanted. Until I got arrested.

Because it was late on a Friday afternoon, Kevin's parking lot was empty. I pulled into the space nearest his office and turned the car off, hardly daring to breathe. I could do this. Too bad I hadn't had time to come up with a disguise. Other than the baker's hat, there wasn't anything handy, and putting that on was a terrible idea.

Sirens wailed.

Uh-oh.

Two police cars tore into the parking lot. Immediately, I hit the start button. Maybe I could—

—get penned in.

Clearly I needed to give the police more credit. They'd had no problem tracking me down.

With a sigh, I rolled down my window. Sheriff Matthews approached, gun drawn.

"Put your hands where I can see them."

I lifted my hands, eyes desperately seeking an escape. Since I didn't want to get shot, there didn't seem to be many options.

"Proton," I muttered.

If he heard me, he ignored the insult. "I'm going to open the door. I want you to get out of the car very, very slowly. Do you understand me?"

"You're a lousy sheriff, and the mayor is evil," I said. "Someday, I hope you both get what you deserve."

He chuckled and reached for my door handle. "Maybe we will, but not today. Aluminum Reynolds, you have the right to remain silent. You have the right—"

THE PACKAGE LOOKED COMPLETELY NORMAL. U.S. Priority Mail medium-sized box, just like my mom used whenever mailing us gifts. Only this cursed "gift" wasn't from my mother at all.

Ugh.

Okay, new plan. Kevin's office was a no-go. But I still needed to get to Amira on Main Street. After I grabbed my keys and got my car headed down the block, I called Rusty.

He answered immediately. "Didn't your powers tell you something like this might happen?"

"You're hilarious. You wouldn't *believe* the day I've had. What did Doug tell you?"

"Enough."

"I would never dream of asking you to pick sides but—"

"You want me to choose you over Doug?" He sounded wary, and I wondered if calling him was a mistake. But it was too late now. He was my best shot.

"Not exactly. Doug's on my side. I already talked to him. He said you'd clear my name."

"Really? When? He just got called away a few minutes ago."

"Oh, not in this reality. Earlier."

Rusty choked. In the background, I heard coughing. A moment later, he said, "You can't say stuff like that when I'm drinking."

"It's been a day. I promise, I'll explain later. But for now, I need to borrow your car. Are you home?"

"I am. I had planned a romantic dinner date with my boyfriend, including his-and-his massages and a specially prepared home-cooked meal."

Now I felt like a jerk. "Let me guess. Doug had to leave suddenly?"

"Why yes, he did! You're so smart."

"There is a time and a place for sarcasm, but this isn't it. Listen. The sheriff thinks I killed Tony. Doug believes I didn't. You know it, too."

"Duh. I was just pushing your buttons. Do you want me to drive your car around, lead the police on a merry chase? That could be fun."

My heart stopped at the thought. After what happened to Tiffaneigh? Nope. No way. Hard pass. "That won't be necessary. Just let me park in your garage for a few hours and use your car. I need to go to the magic shop, and I can't drive down Main Street while the police are looking for me."

"You are aware that Doug will recognize my car, right?"

"Sure, but he's not looking for *you* at the moment." This had to work. I didn't have any other ideas. Kevin's car was both very recognizable and out of state. Gripping the steering wheel, I turned into a residential development and prayed.

Several long seconds later, Rusty said, "You're right. Come on over."

"Great!" I pulled into the driveway. "I'm here! Can you open your garage for me?"

He laughed, and the line went dead. Ten seconds later, the garage door rumbled upward, revealing Rusty's SUV on the right and the space that usually housed Doug's car on the left. Rusty stood in the doorway leading to the house.

Jumping out, I ran to him. He opened his arms, and I dove into them, squeezing like he was my life jacket. It took every ounce of restraint I had not to sob.

He stroked my hair. "Hey. Everything is going to be okay. I've got you. We can get through this together."

My breath hitched. But if I let myself fall apart now, there would be no pulling it back together. I needed to maintain control long enough to ask Amira for help. Finally, I swallowed and stepped back.

"How can I help?" Rusty asked softly. "Do you need a burner phone?"

My best friend worked as a PI, so it didn't surprise me that he'd have a stash of disposable phones around. "You don't happen to have any fingerprint powder, do you? And access to the police database?"

He barked out a laugh. "I wish."

Time was both moving too fast and too slow. I needed to go. Rusty held out his keys, and I kissed his cheek before starting toward his Toyota Highlander.

Halfway across the garage, I stopped. The orb. Although I didn't understand any of this, if Mary had the power to change time and she wanted to hurt me, I couldn't leave the orb unattended in the trunk of my car. I refused to leave the orb in Rusty's garage if there was any possibility of Mary sensing its power and coming to get it. After all, the original plan had been to use the orb to lure her in. It only took a second to grab it—and, on a whim, the bags of supplies from I'll Put a Spell on You. Better to be over-prepared than caught defenseless facing a witch with a vendetta.

Besides, if taking this extra time caused the loop to reset, I'd know to leave everything in my trunk next time. For now, I tossed the bags over to the passenger's seat while climbing into the car.

I paused just long enough to meet Rusty's eyes and cross my arms over my chest in the sign for "love". Then I clicked my seatbelt into place, adjusted the mirrors, put the car into reverse, and drove back toward Main Street.

CHAPTER FOURTEEN

THE UNIVERSE MUST HAVE SMILED on me for a change, because Main Street was empty when I got to the magic shop. I parallel-parked right in front of Amira's place. After confirming no one else was around, I grabbed the package with the baker's hat off the front seat, scrambled out of Rusty's SUV, and raced into I'll Put a Spell on You for the second time that day.

Amira looked up from the counter. "Aly! Did you forget something?"

"Oh, I wish." I held up the box as I flipped the sign to Closed and locked the front door. "When I got home earlier, this thing was on my doorstep. I picked it up, and I've been stuck in a time loop ever since."

"I'm sorry, did you say a time loop?"

"Yeah. I keep finding myself back at the moment I picked up this package."

She eyed it warily. "Will I get sucked into the time loop with you if I touch it?"

"Beats the heck out of me," I said. "This is all very new."

"Fair enough. Have you opened it?"

"Oh, yes." Briefly I explained what happened when I put on the hat.

"Did Olive verify that the hat belongs to Tony?"

I hesitated.

"Aly. You talked to Olive about this, right?"

"Not yet. Before I looped the first time, the police went straight from my house to Missing Pieces. I need to make sure they're gone before I bother her."

"You know those newfangled devices that call people and make a strange ringing noise to alert them? I'm sure she'd meet you somewhere."

"I didn't want to have to put her in the position of lying," I said. "Like I just did to you. Oh, man. I am the worst."

Amira put one hand on my forearm. "Relax. Breathe. It's going to be okay. I've been lying to Doug Matthews since he asked if I believed in magic back in third grade. How can I help? Do you want to trace the hat, see where it came from?"

As if the ghost agreed with her, the lights flickered.

I relaxed a little. "You can do that?"

"I can try." She looked at her watch. "Quickly, though. I have an appointment in an hour."

"This shouldn't take long," I said.

The lights flickered again. Amira looked up and smiled ruefully. "Maybe my ghost wants to help?"

I snorted. "Or maybe the electric company is trying to tell you that you forgot to pay your bill."

"Autopay," she replied.

Amira led me to the back room. She stored some of the more dangerous magical items there and occasionally rented it out for a séance or tarot reading.

She dimmed the lights, lit a sage smudge stick, and told me to wave it in the air over the package for cleansing. While I complied, she mixed a few ingredients in a bowl and carried it to the table containing the package. It looked like sparkly pancake mix.

Amira directed me to shake the hat out of the package and place the box beside it on the table to avoid adding her impressions to either of them. Then she took a pinch of the mix from the bowl and tossed it in the air above the empty box.

She wrinkled her nose.

"Anything?" I asked.

She shook her head. "Not at all. Maybe it's been through too many people? Or maybe whoever sent it used some kind of psychic protection?"

"Why would they do that?"

"So you couldn't track them. Whoever did this must know what you can do. Or what your friends can do."

A fair point. I pressed my lips together, and Amira repeated the procedure over the baker's hat. This time, she grimaced.

"What's wrong?" I asked.

"There's a thick layer of spells on this hat," she said. "I can probably sort through them, but this is more Mom's territory. I should call to see if she can walk me through it."

"I've been trying to reach Kevin ever since the first time I reset. The calls never go through." I swallowed hard, refusing to consider the possibilities. "His phone must be off."

"I'm sure it is," Amira said. "Or the spell is preventing you from talking to him. Mom would know, but I'm guessing we can't call her either."

At that, I tried Mrs. Patel's number, but it went straight to voicemail. I couldn't decide whether that made me feel better or worse.

Amira continued to focus on the baker's hat for several minutes. I watched, but didn't have any clue what she was doing. Sprinkling some stuff, saying some words. Some of them English; many sounded like Latin.

Then she shifted her focus back to the box. After a minute, she sat up straight in her chair. "A-ha!"

"A-ha? That sounds good."

"Sort of. I can see the person who delivered it. But on second thought, it doesn't tell us much."

"What do you mean?"

She waved her hand over the cardboard box, and the smoke from the incense came together into a man's face. He was about our age. Cute. He had spiky hair, chiseled cheekbones, and a wide smile. "I know this guy."

"I've never seen him before in my life," I said. "Is he a witch? A murderer?"

"Unfortunately, neither. He's a delivery driver who lives in Willow Falls. We matched on a dating app about a month ago. Someone must've paid him to take the box to you. He probably doesn't know anything about who sent it."

She looked so sad, I wanted to make her feel better. "At least he's nice to look at. Did you go out?"

"Oh, goodness no. He thought Pluto got its name from being shaped like the cartoon dog."

It took a minute for that to process. "He thought dwarf planet Pluto received its name from a Disney character? And that it was shaped like a dog?"

"Yeah. Good thing he's cute." She waved her hand again, and the image dissipated. "Sorry I can't be more helpful. Want me to head down to Missing Pieces and see if the police are gone on the way to my showing? If so, I can give Olive the hat."

"Thanks. Let me help you clean up first."

When I stood, I swayed on my feet. This whole spellcasting thing had made me woozy. Or maybe it wasn't the magic. It took me a minute to realize that the pie air in here had changed. It seemed thicker, maybe. Darker? A byproduct of the spell. It was making me sleepy. Or maybe the day I'd had made me sleepy. All of a sudden, my eyelids weighed a thousand pounds.

To clear my head, I forced myself to wander around the

room. After a minute I paused and lifted my nose. Then I sniffed the air.

"Do you smell anything?" I asked.

"It's just the sulfur," she said. "Or the incense. Sometimes these spells get pungent."

Something still seemed off, but I didn't have a better explanation. "Yeah, okay. I guess."

"I know you've had a rough day, but everything is fine," she said. "I've done this a hundred times. The sulfur is smelly, but it's totally safe. Anyway, it doesn't matter. We're done. I'm sorry, Aly."

If possible, the sulfur smelled even worse after I blew out the incense. "You sure we can't find out anything else?"

She pressed her lips together. "I don't think so. The hat has spells on it, like I said. The only thing I can say is, I don't think it is specifically causing the time loop, which is to say that destroying it probably won't fix anything."

"Oooh. Can we try?" If nothing else, mutilating the hat would help me release some frustration. I was all for it.

"Maybe if it weren't evidence in a murder investigation."

A valid point, although if setting the thing on fire would unravel the whole spell and put me back on a normal time-line, I would risk it. "Anything else?"

"What is most interesting isn't what the spells are, but who placed them. I don't know if you're aware of this, but most magics leave fingerprints. A unique signature. You could even say, a calling card. I've seen this signature before. These spells were placed by a witch I know. More importantly, a witch *you* know."

"Mary." It wasn't a question.

"You don't seem surprised."

"She's the only person I could think of who would have both the power to do something like this and a strong desire to mess with me."

Amira pondered my words. "Yeah. That Venn diagram is a complete circle."

"In some ways, I wanted it to be someone else," I said. "But it makes sense. We're planning big things for the anniversary of Katrina's death. Maybe she is, too. What do we do now?"

"I'll do some research. Meanwhile, maybe you can get time back to normal if you can figure out what she wants you to do."

"She wants me to give her my nephew, which will happen over my dead body."

"Can we lure her in and bind her while you're in the time loop? Tonight instead of in the morning?"

"There's no way for me to get Emma here until tomorrow. If I can't call Kevin or your mom, I can't call her," I said. "Do you think you can work it on your own?"

"I'm sorry, but no. Even with the orb, we need her."

My rising hopes plummeted down to the earth. Emma couldn't help until tomorrow. Mary had put me in a time loop that wouldn't let me get to tomorrow. Was it getting warm in here? I was starting to get light-headed from the stress of it all. With a moan, I sank down into my chair and buried my head in my hands.

Amira squeezed my shoulder. "It'll be okay. I can drive out to Willow Falls later and talk to her if the phones won't work."

She gathered up the stuff we'd used and went to wash her hands at a sink in the attached bathroom while I blew out the rest of the candles. By the time I finished, the room stunk so badly, I turned to look for a window. Nothing. I guess that made sense since this used to be a storeroom. Amira needed to control the light for her spells. She really needed to install a vent or add some fans, though.

Waving one hand to clear the air, I went for the door. My eyes were watering from the smoke. This was terrible.

Throwing the door open, I was preparing to dart through it when a blast of heat hit me. Instead of dissipating, the smoke grew stronger.

What the—?

My first instinct was to investigate, but there was nowhere to go. Flames filled the other end of the hallway. Taking two steps back into the storeroom, I slammed the door and dropped to the floor, croaking Amira's name.

"What's wrong?" She coughed as she approached. "We need to air this place out."

"Stop!" I yelped. Amira jumped away from the door as if I'd slapped her. Quickly, I said, "Fire. The whole store is on fire."

"What? How could that happen?" The color drained from her face. "Oh, no. The flickering lights. My dad told me it was an electrical problem. I thought I was so cool, having a ghost in a magic shop!"

If we didn't get out of here, whoever rebuilt the store would have two legit ghosts in their new endeavor. My mind raced for any means of escape.

"Is there a window in the bathroom?" I asked.

She shook her head. "We're going to have to go through the door."

"There's no path that way," I said. "The hallway is a tunnel of flames. What about a back door?"

"The only way to get to it is down that hall." Her eyes filled with tears. "We're trapped."

"Oh, Amira. I'm so sorry. I should never have come here."

"It's not your fault. I should have called an electrician weeks ago."

I racked my brain, but at the end of the day, there was only one solution. When Tiffaneigh died, time reset. If the fire consumed me, I should bounce back to the front foyer. I had to believe it.

Amira's eyes narrowed. "Whatever you're thinking, I don't like it."

"I know," I said. "But it'll be okay."

Standing up straight, I took a deep breath. Then I opened the door and trudged toward the flames. Amira screamed my name. I pushed her inside the room and slammed the door behind me. I needed to do this, and there was no reason for her to go with me.

Element one was hydrogen. Element two was carbon.

Time to go.

Halfway down the hall, a beam cracked overhead. I looked up. Panic flared in my throat. My eyes welled with tears.

Then the gray mist descended.

CHAPTER FIFTEEN

THE PACKAGE LOOKED COMPLETELY NORMAL. U.S. Priority Mail medium-sized box, just like my mom used whenever mailing us gifts.

Kyle's *Highlights Kids* magazine in my other hand, my phone showing 2:57 p.m. Yet again.

Oh, thank goodness. I never wanted to die in a fire again. That was absolutely awful. Remembering made it hard to breathe. So much that I wasted precious seconds going to get a drink of water before heading to my car.

By the time I set the glass on the kitchen counter, I felt a little better. Something Amira said before came to me. If I destroyed the hat, would I end the spell?

Was it even evidence of a crime?

No need to convince me. I would surely get a grim satisfaction from getting rid of this thing. First, I pulled our largest metal mixing bowl out from the cupboard and set it on the middle of the island. Far from any walls or curtains that might be scorched.

On second thought, I moved it into the sink. Less flammable, immediate access to water.

Rather than cutting open the package, I grabbed the meat

tenderizer and whacked the box a few times. That felt good. The box went into the trash, the hat in the bowl. I grabbed a bottle of Kevin's most expensive brandy from the top shelf, with barely a twinge at what it cost. After dumping the entire thing over the hat, I lit a match.

"Please, please, let this work." I said the words aloud like a prayer.

Then I dropped the match into the bowl.

CHAPTER SIXTEEN

SO MUCH FOR THAT HYPOTHESIS. The unopened package containing a presumably unburnt chef's hat was in my hand, in the front hall. At two-freaking-fifty-seven.

Time to get out of here. The police were on their way, and now I wanted to fix this mess more than I wanted to wait and insult them when they arrived. Yet again, I ran to my car, punched the garage door opener, threw the shifter into reverse, and slammed onto the accelerator.

My next move was both risky and obvious. Amira's spell told me that Mary placed the spell on the baker's hat and who delivered it. I could guess why, but did the hat really belong to Tony? How did the vision get onto the hat in the first place? Maybe someone else hit Tony with a rolling pin and Mary changed their face? There was one person nearby who could answer at least one of those questions.

Going to Olive might prove to be a mistake, but I'd already made several of those today. It didn't seem to matter. If she could say or do anything to shed some light on what was happening, it would be worth—

—seeing her die? Watching her get arrested? Oh, dear.

No. I could do this. It wasn't real. Taking a deep breath, I recited the elements of the periodic table all the way to Main Street. I just needed to grab her and get out before the police arrived. We had maybe ten minutes. Not nearly enough time to swap cars with Rusty.

Missing Pieces was only a mile from home, so even taking a circuitous route out of my neighborhood, I arrived a few minutes later and parked in the alley beside the store. Not in an actual space, but it's not like getting towed would be the worst thing that happened to me today.

Olive took one look at my face and moved toward the front of the shop, changing the sign on the door to "Closed" and turning the lights off. "Come on. Let's go upstairs."

"Won't people wonder why the store is closed in the middle of the day? Olive, listen, the police are looking for me. They're on their way."

"Before you came along, I shut the shop for lunch almost every day. People will live without me for ten minutes. Now, let's go." Not giving me a chance to object further, she put one arm around my shoulders and steered us toward the upstairs apartment she shared with her wife, Maria.

The second we got into the back room, I dug in my heels and started talking. "Stop. There's not a lot of time, but we have to go."

"That's what we're doing. I'm taking you upstairs for some tea."

"We can't go upstairs. It's not safe," I insisted. Taking a deep breath, I continued, "Something is happening to me, Olive. I don't know what it is, but the police are looking for me and Tony the baker is dead and then Tiffaneigh died in a car accident and then I ran over Mrs. Chang's cat and I screamed at Sheriff Matthews and Jeff got stuck as a rabbit and Amira's store burned down—" I broke off with a wail, burying my face in my hands.

Olive wrapped her arms around me, enveloping me in her familiar lavender patchouli scent. "It's going to be okay."

"How?"

"I don't know quite yet. That's a lot of information. You ran over a cat? When was there a fire? I didn't hear anything."

I sniffled. "Not in this reality."

"That makes perfect sense," Olive said dryly. "Why don't you start at the beginning?"

After blinking the tears out of my vision, I went back to the first time I opened the front door, from finding the package with the baker's hat to everything that happened since. Finally, I wound up with, "Jeff went into the bakery for me to look around, because he could get into tight spaces. He got stuck. He's okay now because time reset, but it freaked me out."

"Do you have the hat? I'd like to examine it."

Well, duh. That would have been a brilliant idea. Bring the hat to the person who would confirm it belonged to Tony without the need for pesky DNA tests. I closed my eyes and inhaled deeply.

"Is that a no?" Olive asked.

"I forgot it in my car," I said sheepishly. "Let's go get it."

"Nonsense. I'll get it. You stay here."

"You don't have any reason to be poking around my car," I protested. "I can't drag you further into this."

"I'm already involved," she countered.

"True, but…" I didn't know how to put this into words. Every time someone had helped me since this spell began, something bad happened to them. Yes, I realized Olive was in danger from the second I showed up here, but I didn't have to further jeopardize her by sending her out to steal evidence. "It's not necessary. I know the hat is Tony's. I had a vision of him when I put it on."

"That's right. And in this vision, you saw yourself—killing him?"

I nodded. "But that's ridiculous, right? My visions show the past. I never see the future. At first I thought it was a future vision of me killing Tony. Which I wouldn't do. But then Sheriff Matthews and Doug showed up, and they seem convinced Tony's already dead."

"Could that be part of the spell?"

"Maybe? Amira saw Mary's magical fingerprints on the hat. But I don't know the details. Did she fabricate the whole thing? Did she change an existing scene? All I know is, I didn't do it." I paused. "Can Mary conjure up a false vision?"

"I don't know about that, but I bet she could send you one of Priscilla's."

Mary and Katrina's cousin had a power similar to mine, but instead of seeing past events, she got images of the future. At least once that we were aware of, she'd used those visions to help Katrina avoid injury. Too bad it wasn't enough to save her.

A heavy sigh escaped me. Katrina was gone, and I needed to focus on what was happening right now. Then a thought hit me.

"Could Mary have possessed me? Could she have forced me to kill Tony before I left the bakery?"

Olive thought for a minute before shaking her head. "I don't think so. One of the first tenets of witchcraft is to do no harm. While it might be possible for Mary to gather the power to possess you—she has shown a lot of strength, after all—I don't think she could overcome your natural morality to make you commit cold-blooded murder."

"Even if he was being a total jerk?"

Olive smiled indulgently. "Not even then. You're too good a person."

Back to square one.

"Have you talked to Kevin? He might know more about Mary and Priscilla's abilities than we do."

"Not about this. He was supposed to call me once he checked into the hotel." I thought for a minute. "We spoke right after I left the bakery. That was before the time loop started. Sheriff Matthews was on the street outside. After I looped the first time, I tried to call him, but I dropped my phone. Never noticed whether he picked up."

"And since then…?"

"Amira and I tried to call her mom and Kevin. We couldn't get through. We thought the spell was somehow blocking our efforts."

"You may be right," Olive said. "The good news is, that means Kevin, Kyle, and Mrs. Patel are probably perfectly safe from the spell."

"But not from Mary, who is also outside the spell."

"Right," she said.

"How do I find her?"

Olive moved toward the back door. "To start, let's go to your car. I'll do a reading on the hat while you drive us across the county line. My guess is that Mary doesn't have the power to loop more than the geographical limits of Shady Grove. We might be able to get outside the spell and warn Kevin from there."

That made sense, except for one thing. "You stay here. I can't involve you deeper in this."

She laughed. "Don't be silly. You most certainly can. Let's go."

We swung by my car exactly long enough for me to retrieve the currently unopened package (presumably) holding Tony's hat and hand it to Olive.

"You should move your car, Aly. You might get towed."

I shrugged. "It doesn't matter at this point."

She opened her mouth to argue but got distracted turning the package over and over in her fingers. "It's still sealed. How do you know there's a baker's hat inside?"

"Magic," I said dryly. "I've opened it like eight times today. Go ahead."

I slid into the front passenger seat of Olive's car and ducked down below the window while she walked around to the driver's side. Once we were settled, she opened the package. As expected, a white baker's hat slid out. She didn't even have to put it on the way I did.

"You're right. It belongs to Tony," she said.

"Told you so."

Ignoring me, she put the car into gear. We drove away from Missing Pieces. Since the Vermont border was close, she got on a state highway heading east. With every passing mile, I felt better.

Until we got to the edge of Shady Grove County, and a now-familiar gray mist descended.

CHAPTER SEVENTEEN

SO MUCH FOR THAT PLAN. Apparently, Olive and I weren't going anywhere together. I could try sending her across the county line alone, but I suspected she wouldn't make it. I didn't particularly want to know what would happen.

Back to Missing Pieces. This time after I explained everything, I asked Olive to take me to Tony's house. Maybe Mary had planted something there, a sign or a message for me. I didn't know where Tony lived, so getting this information from Olive now would help if time looped again. Maybe I could come back without involving her next time.

Tony lived in a modest, two-family colonial-style house about halfway between Kevin's place and the golf course. According to Olive, his sister lived in the upstairs unit, with Tony below. A realtor's sign stood out front. My inner scientist wondered how much force it took to drive a wooden stake through the layers of snow and ice into the frozen ground.

That thought faded away when I realized I recognized the realtor smiling out of the corrugated plastic. Todd LaCroix worked in Willow Falls, where I'd met him earlier this year at Mary's house. Long story.

Mentally, I reminded myself of his name and firm since chances were any picture taken with my phone wouldn't remain if this time loop reset.

Huh. Interesting hypothesis. One worth testing.

Lifting my phone, I turned to Olive. "Say cheese!"

"Why? What on earth are you doing?"

"Just checking something," I said as I tucked the phone away. "It doesn't matter."

According to Amira, Todd planned to do showings today starting at four. They may or may not all be here—he likely listed more than one house at a time. She didn't mention if her appointment was the only one.

Olive and I needed to proceed as if Todd would be here in about half an hour. We didn't have a lot of time. Hopefully it would be enough.

Before walking up to the house, we studied the street. Apparently Tony's neighbors were either all at work or all hunkered down, avoiding the snow. Every driveway had been cleared, and no cars were parked on any of them. A shiny, white BMW sat parked in front of a house on the other side of the street. No salt on the outside, so it must have been recently washed. There didn't appear to be anyone inside the car. No one to see us breaking and entering. Perfect.

As we approached the porch, I examined the outside. White paint. Window boxes with flowers that were starting to wilt, but must have been pretty when planted.

"Tony doesn't strike me as a flower box kind of guy," I said.

Olive snorted. "I'm sure he doesn't. Donna made those."

Right.

Leaning past Olive, I pushed the doorbell and held it. Even though I didn't expect anyone to answer, Tony could have had a roommate or a partner or even a dog walker. I didn't know him at all. "We should go talk to her. Maybe she knows something."

"She won't be here. Donna moved in with her fiancé a couple of months ago."

Interesting. Was Tony moving because his sister left? Was he happy about that? Maybe he and Donna had argued.

I tilted my head toward the house but heard nothing moving inside. Finally, I reached for the knob.

"What are you doing?" Olive asked.

"No one is here. The police think I killed Tony. Since burglary isn't as bad as murder, I'm going in to gather clues."

"Yes, I know that," Olive said. "You're not wearing gloves. You'll leave fingerprints everywhere."

"So?"

"Fingerprints are evidence! You've never had any reason to be in Tony's house. What if the time loop doesn't reset?"

I thought about it for a minute. "I'll concede the point, but if I was supposed to go to jail, we wouldn't be having this conversation. I've been arrested twice today."

To my surprise, when I twisted the knob, the front door swung open easily. As did the one to the upstairs unit. Olive and I exchanged a look.

"Guess we're trying to buy you a house," she said, leaning into the hallway. "Hello? Anyone here?"

No response. After a moment, she went into the upstairs hall and shouted again. Silence.

"Maybe the realtor left it open for a showing?" I said. Weird, when the prospective buyers could have used the lock-box. "Or he ran out to get something?"

"As long as he's not here to have you arrested, I don't care."

I gestured through the second doorway. "Are you ready?"

"This will be faster if we split up," Olive said. "If you find the realtor, pretend you're looking to buy."

Although part of me was afraid to let her out of my sight, it made sense.

Since I was standing in front of the door on the left, I

pushed it. The wooden door swung open to reveal highly polished floors and a stairway leading upstairs. It also went down, presumably to a basement. Moving quickly, I climbed to the upper landing and entered the apartment.

Nice place. A decent-sized entry, with a seat for guests removing boots and hanging jackets and scarves. Beside the door, a sign welcomed me into the home.

To the left, a large L-shaped couch took up most of the room, facing a television over a fireplace. Crouching, I peered through the screen to find a couple of artfully arranged fake logs. Whatever I was expecting to find, it wasn't there. No ashes, no singed bits of evidence. None of the things Angela Lansbury certainly would have spotted if she were here.

Beyond the living room was the kitchen. No pots, no pans, not a single mug or crumb to be found. Everything beautifully staged, but I couldn't expect to find any clues about Tony's death up here.

I took a quick tour of the rest of the place, but it was pristine. No clothes in the closets, no toiletries in the bathroom cabinet, nothing but a roll of cheap toilet paper under the sink. On my way out, something made me pause. I cocked my head, listening. Was Olive calling me? Surely she understood that since I was wanted for murder, she shouldn't run around yelling my name.

"Olive?"

"Aly! Come here." Her voice sounded strangled.

"Where are you?"

"Bottom of the stairs."

When I returned to the landing, I found her waiting by the exterior door. Her face was white, eyes wide open.

"What's going on? Why didn't you come up?"

"I can't right now." She placed one hand on her chest and took a deep breath.

The stairs weren't that steep. Olive was in decent shape. Exploring the house shouldn't take this much out of her.

"What's wrong? Does Tony have a mouse problem down there?"

"I wish." She shuddered. "There's a dead man in the basement. It's not Tony."

Whoa.

Of all the things I'd expected to find here, someone *other* than Tony dead hadn't even made the list.

Element twenty-six was iron. Element twenty-seven was cobalt. Element twenty-eight was nickel.

Once I could breathe normally, I tapped my foot and checked the time on my phone.

"What are you doing?" Olive asked.

"I'm waiting for the time loop to reset. Whenever someone with me has died today, it ended the loop, and I wound up back in my front hall. Should be any second now." Impatiently, I glanced at the display on my phone. Come on…

Olive's voice broke into my thoughts. "Why would it reset now? I didn't kill that man."

A valid point. We had no idea how long that person had been dead, but it probably didn't have anything to do with me. Yes, it was weird for him to be in Tony's house, but maybe that was part of the puzzle I needed to solve.

If this person presented a clue as to what was happening, maybe we were supposed to find him. Maybe the same person killed Tony and the guy in the basement! (Was that person Mary? While her fingerprints were all over the spell, indiscriminately murdering someone didn't seem like her style.) Or maybe he was an intruder and Tony stopped him before getting killed himself. Only one way to find out.

"Lead the way."

Olive turned and went back to the downstairs apartment. This. This was what I'd expected Tony's apartment to look like. A leather couch sat under the window, with a massive armchair sitting perpendicular. The seats shared an end table. Across from the couch, he'd hung the largest TV I'd ever seen in my life. If Olive and I weren't on our way to examine a dead body, I would have stopped to measure it. It was practically a movie screen.

He'd hung some photographs of the most amazing-looking cakes. One was decorated like a spaceship, another a perfect replica of Luigi from Super Mario Bros. These were almost too gorgeous to eat. There were six photographs, and I strongly suspected Tony had baked each of them. How sad that such enormous talent was gone.

When we reached the basement door, I paused.

"You don't have to go back in there. I can look on my own," I said to Olive. She still looked pretty distressed.

"No, no. It's fine. I just…" She closed her eyes for a moment, took a deep breath, and exhaled slowly before opening them. "Neither of us can go in. The staircase collapsed."

"Should we have gone in through Donna's place instead?"

"Do you have any reason to believe the staircase there is more sound or safer than this one used to be?"

"Now that you mention it? No."

She continued, "I still don't want your fingerprints in the basement. I just needed to show you who I found. It's time to go."

Leaning past her, I looked inside. She'd left the light on, and while it wasn't terribly bright, I could see enough to make out the lack of a staircase where it should be, attached to the landing. Below us, a man wearing an expensive suit lay face down on a pile of rubble.

I wasn't positive, but the cut of the expensive-looking suit and the straight blond hair looked familiar. "I think that's Todd Lacroix."

"Why is that name familiar?"

"He's on the sign outside. This guy looks like the realtor."

She narrowed her eyes for a moment, studying him. "You may be right."

"I need to see if he's okay."

"Don't touch him!" Olive reminded me.

"How do you know he's dead if you didn't check? Maybe he's only unconscious." I turned away so I could head back to Donna's apartment, although I still didn't love the idea of putting my weight on her basement stairs after this set collapsed.

Olive put her head on my arm. "Trust me. He's dead. Look at the way his head is lying. The human body doesn't turn that way."

She had a point. How did this happen? Unless Tony had a major termite problem, the staircase shouldn't just tumble down. Crouching, I used the flashlight on my phone to examine the place where the stairs once connected with the wall. Broken off pieces of wood still stuck out. While I'd expect it to be jagged, instead, the wood just stopped. Carefully, I ran my hand along one of them. It was perfectly smooth most of the way down, as if cut. The end was splintered, jagged, as expected.

"Ow!" Pulling my hand back, I stuck one finger in my mouth.

"Great. Now you've left blood at the crime scene," Olive said.

"Sorry. But I had to check. This was no accident," I said. "That staircase was sabotaged. We need to look at the other side. And look here!"

I pointed at the wall, where the railing must have once been attached. Now there was nothing but screw holes at even intervals.

"I'm not letting you touch anything else down there or anything else in this house. We need to get out and call the police."

"You didn't call already?" She was normally so clear-headed and practical. Her delay surprised me.

"I was in shock. Unlike you, I don't find dead bodies every day."

Ouch.

"That's not fair. I've only actually *found* two. And one was fake."

"Let's not argue semantics, shall we? Let's get you out of here, and then we'll call from a safe location far, far away."

Olive turned and strode back through the kitchen, headed for the front door. Suddenly, she shrieked and flailed her arms.

"Olive?"

It was too late. I stepped forward, but the kitchen mat had slipped on the shiny tile floor. She skidded forward. Tried to catch her balance. She leaned back. I lunged for her. The rug moved to the right, toward the center of the room. Olive went left with a yell.

My fingertips brushed the air as she went past me. Then her head hit the kitchen countertop. A sickening crack filled the air. She fell to the floor.

Still screaming, I darted to her side, barely managing to avoid falling myself. My hands moved frantically to her neck, feeling for a pulse.

Nothing.

Too late.

In the blink of an eye, Olive was gone.

The world swam before my eyes. I couldn't breathe. I could—

CHAPTER EIGHTEEN

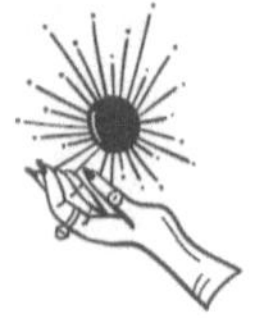

—-BREATHE.

My screams died when I found myself once again inside Kevin's entryway. Heart still pounding, I forced myself to calm down by reciting the periodic table backwards. When my mind finally stilled, I looked at the object being squished in a death grip between my palms.

The package looked completely normal. A standard U.S. Priority Mail medium-sized box, just like my mom used whenever mailing us gifts. It shook in my hands. As I stared at it, a tear plopped down onto the cardboard. A tear that started in Tony's house.

After that loop, I needed a minute. I didn't care if time reset forever, as long as I never had to watch Olive die again. The noise in my throat that had started before time looped continued oozing out, an unending moan.

Poor Olive.

I knew I shouldn't have gone to her for help. But she was my rock. Not being able to count on her threw my world off its axis even more than being forced to repeat this stupid day over and over. I had to fix this. I needed to get to tomorrow so I could do the spell.

My head was still spinning. This was no good. I couldn't drive. The police would be here soon; I couldn't stay. Where to go?

I'd been reasonably safe at the next-door neighbor's house. I moved through the house to the next yard, careful to avoid leaving a trail in the pristine snow of the front yard.

Once I'd secreted myself in their basement for the third— or was it fourth? —time, I sank to the ground. The dam holding back my tears broke, and I braced myself for the flood. I didn't know how much time passed before I finally got myself under control.

It's not real. It's not real. She's fine. Tiffaneigh is fine. The cat is fine. Jeff is a person, not a bunny. Amira's store is intact. Everyone is fine.

Element one was hydrogen. Once I went through all 118 elements of the periodic table three times, I felt somewhat human. Sheriff Matthews and/or Doug would likely come search here soon, but it didn't matter right now. Until I could pull myself together, nothing mattered.

I needed to talk to Sam. He always reassured me. Granted, I'd never called him after witnessing his mother's death, but it would be better for both of us if I didn't mention that minor fact. She was alive in this reality, and that was the important thing.

Pulling my phone out of my pocket, I swiped to my recent video calls and tapped on Sam's name. A moment later, his handsome face came into view. I loved that face. Loved that brown hair, the strong jaw that usually had a hint of stubble. I also loved his quick, crooked smile, but that dropped when he took in my features. It hadn't occurred to me that I must look like a total wreck.

"Aly? What's wrong? Are we still on for this weekend?"

I'd thought I'd been all cried out, but those words were my undoing. A second flood burst out, while I tried desperately to say anything coherent. Sam's image bounced all over the place, the background blurry.

Finally, I got myself under control. "Where are you?"

The bouncing slowed, and Sam's features became clear once more.

"Near campus," he said. "I was walking around the park when you called, but there's a band practicing or something. I wanted to get somewhere quiet. Now that I can hear you, let's start over. What's wrong?"

Since I didn't know how much time I had in this world, I launched into my story. To his credit, Sam didn't once look like he doubted me. Having a mother with magical powers and a psychic girlfriend had made him pretty unflappable.

"Okay, so you're caught in a time loop. Have you asked Mom about it?"

My throat closed up.

"Never mind, I don't want to know," he said. "How can I help? Should I come to Shady Grove now? I can skip tonight's lecture."

Someone yelled. I jumped, but no one was there. The voice came from behind Sam.

"Everything okay?"

"Yeah, sorry. I seem to have taken a shortcut through a construction site. Which isn't my fault. Half the city is just scaffolding. Back to you. Need me to pick you up?"

On the one hand, that could be extremely helpful. On the other hand, getting in the car with someone else had gone horribly wrong every time I'd tried it today. Other than offering moral support, I wasn't sure what Sam could do at the moment. He could help me reason through my options just as easily—and more safely—from New York City.

Funny. If someone had told me yesterday that our small town was more dangerous than one of the most populated cities in the world, I'd have laughed. But now I knew how dangerous Shady Grove could be.

"No, thanks. I like knowing you're safe."

"Same. Which is why I really think I should—"

Someone yelled again. A screeching filled the air, so loud it sounded like it was in the next room. Sam looked up.

Something slammed into him. The phone crashed to the ground. All I could see was sky.

"Sam? Are you there?"

No answer.

More voices. Feet pounding. And seconds later, a siren. Oh, no.

A shadow passed over the screen, and a second later I found myself staring into a stranger's face. Pale skin, a smattering of freckles, red hair with a touch of gray, and hazel eyes. He wore a construction hat, and my stomach dropped to the floor.

"What's happening? Where's Sam?" With each word, I sounded more hysterical.

"I'm so sorry," the man said.

"What? Why?" I both desperately needed to hear his answer and never wanted him to speak the words.

"A beam. The chain snapped. We lost it. We said to stand clear... I'm sorry. I guess he didn't hear us. Oh, man." The man ran one hand through his hair. "I'm so sorry, miss. Do you know his name?"

"Sam," I choked out. "Is he alive?"

Eyes brimming with tears, the man shook his head.

A wail escaped me.

No. Not Sam.

I'd lost too many people I cared about today. Tiffaneigh, Olive. Now Sam, too. I couldn't do this anymore. This spell was just cruel.

Without another word, I hung up on the man who still looked horrified to be talking to me. I had to find Mary. I had to get out of this mess. Then I dialed Mary's number.

"Aly? How are you, dear?"

Dear? Oh, yes. She was definitely the one responsible.

"You're going to pay for this," I hissed. "How could you be so cruel? If you want to kill me, kill me. Stop making me witness the deaths of everyone I love."

"You're being melodramatic. They're fine."

"What do you mean, they're fine?" My voice rose with every word. "I watched them die!"

"When time resets, everything rewinds to the beginning. If you find your way out, dead people stay dead. But if you loop again—viola! It's a miracle!"

"If that's true, why is Tony still dead?"

She laughed. "Oh, that's the beauty of this spell, isn't it? Figure that one out, and you'll save everyone."

What did that even mean? The spell started when the hat arrived. Tony was alive when I left the bakery. I had no idea when Tony died. How could I avoid starting the spell? It's not like I could teleport on over to the bakery to save Tony's life.

Clearly, talking to Mary wasn't going to tell me anything useful.

"I am going to solve this, and then I will make sure you never come near any of us again. You're going to jail for so long, your grandchildren will be on parole."

Dropping the phone, I stomped toward the basement stairs. Still furious, I raced upstairs and out the front door, driven by pure rage. When I got to the front lawn, the police cars were exactly where I remembered them from earlier. One in the driveway, one on the street. No sign of either police officer.

Looking up at the sky, I screamed.

And screamed.

And kept screaming, until finally, Doug came to arrest me. This time, I welcomed the gray mist.

CHAPTER NINETEEN

THE PACKAGE LOOKED COMPLETELY NORMAL. U.S. Priority Mail medium-sized box, just like my mom used whenever mailing us gifts.

Ugh. This whole day was so stupid. Not even a day. The same terrible hours, over and over.

This time, I was going to move quickly yet responsibly to get out of the house before the police arrived. In my car, with my coat and my phone. The key was to get as far away as I could within a few minutes. Once I got out of the danger zone, I could figure out my next step.

Yet again, I raced for my car and dove inside. I hung a right at the corner, moving away from Mrs. Chang's cat. My eyes stayed glued to the road. By the time sirens came into range, I was out of our neighborhood and almost halfway to Main Street.

The second I felt safe, I used Siri to call Sam, my fingers squeezing the steering wheel until he picked up.

"Aly? Is everything okay?" he asked.

A huge wave of relief left me unable to speak. Even though I'd known he shouldn't be dead—even though Mary had told me—I'd been so scared. A knot in my chest loosened until finally, I could breathe.

"No, things are not okay. Listen, I can't explain now, but I need you to swear on your life not to walk through any construction zones today. Or tomorrow. Or… ever. Never again. I mean it."

It was a testament to how much this man trusted me that he didn't laugh. "Uh, sure."

"I am dead serious."

"I know, and I promise. Can I help?"

"Not now. Be safe. I love you. I'll call you as soon as I can."

"I love you, too." Concern filled his voice. "Be careful, Aly."

After promising I would, I ended the call and turned my full attention back to my dilemma. Where was I supposed to go? Kevin couldn't help, Olive couldn't help, I couldn't even use Sam as a shoulder to lean on. What about Emma? I'd started to walk to her place earlier but changed my mind after realizing it would take forever. Now I had wheels!

Mind made up, I turned the car toward the county line. The first time I'd lived this stupid day, Tiffaneigh's scanner had said the police were looking for me on Main Street and at major outlets like the train stations and airport—all of which were miles and miles south of here. She hadn't said anything about them watching the roads out of Shady Grove, and considering how small the force was, that should mean they weren't.

Still, I hardly dared breathe as I steered very clear of what constituted our "downtown" area. Finally, my body started to relax when the "Now Leaving Shady Grove" sign came into view. Without even thinking about it, my foot pressed on the accelerator. My tires gobbled up the pavement.

The sign flew by.

And the gray mist appeared. Oh, fluorine. I'd completely forgotten what happened when Olive and I tried to leave town earlier.

The road faded into nothingness, and my whispered curse went with it.

CHAPTER TWENTY

THE PACKAGE LOOKED COMPLETELY NORMAL. U.S. Priority Mail medium-sized box, just like my mom used whenever mailing gifts to me or Kevin or Kyle. Mostly Kyle. So much stuff for Kyle.

Argh! Balling my hands into fists, I took one moment to punch the air as hard as possible. The only thing I accomplished was spinning in a circle. Time to go. Grab the hat, head for the car. Garage door up, garage door down, avoid the cat. Drive where?

Apparently I couldn't leave town. Now what?

Maybe the thing to do was go back to Tony's house and call the police. They could look for evidence. Finding Todd's body after being seen at the bakery made me look even more suspicious, though. I needed to get some answers before calling more attention on myself. Did Tony kill his realtor before going to work and getting murdered?

When I saw Tony, he'd seemed unusually cranky, even for him. I supposed that could be related to having just murdered his realtor, but—who would leave a body in their basement and go to work like nothing happened? Especially when the deceased was supposed to be showing the place to potential buyers and would get found any minute. There was no love lost between me and Tony, but even I could admit he seemed smarter than that.

Did the same person want them both dead? Would the police think that person was me? Did someone want to frame Tony for murder? If so, killing him seemed like a weird way to do it. None of this made any sense.

Or maybe Todd's death had nothing to do with Tony at all. Maybe someone wanted to kill Todd, and he just happened to be in Tony's house.

A groan escaped me. That theory left me at square one and offered no insight into getting out of this time loop, so I decided to ignore it. At the moment, I had bigger fish to fry. Unfortunately, I also had zero ideas where to go or what to do next.

There was one person no one would expect me to seek for help in an emergency. Especially not an emergency that came with a powerful need for discretion. But that someone would know if anyone hated Tony enough to kill him.

Decision made, I set a course for the Shady Grove Golf Club. Yes, even the fanciest and most exclusive place in town stuck a pun in its name. I loved this place, and I really wanted to keep living here rather than in the state prison.

Before the manicured lawns came into view, I swung around the corner and drove a few blocks. My car pulled to a halt in front of a pink house that always made me think of Pepto Bismol. Parking on the street would help me make a quick exit if necessary. Also, only a line of hedges separated these houses from the golf course. That provided an extra escape option out the back door.

Summoning all of my nerve, I moved toward the front porch. My knuckles had barely connected with the light pink wood when the door swung away from me. Luckily, some people lived with their noses pressed to the windows and never took long to answer a knock.

"Aluminum! It's always a pleasure."

"Hi, Thelma."

Before me stood retired soap opera actress and Shady Grove's one and only celebrity, Thelma Reyes. She'd grown up spending summers in town with her aunt and moved here permanently about two decades ago after leaving her show, *As the Hospital Guides Our Lives*. As far as I knew, she hadn't worked a day since, but she still loved to be the center of attention.

Every time the town hosted a function, Thelma could be counted on to be front and center, especially if a microphone or press might be involved. She knew everything about everyone, and she was happy to share.

Many people would question the wisdom of seeking advice on beating a murder rap from the town's gossip. Including me, actually. But there were two major benefits to this plan. First, if things went wrong, the timeline should reset and Thelma would never know I'd been here. Second, if anyone could tell me who would want to kill Tony and/or Todd, she stood in front of me dressed like she was headed to the Oscars.

With those thoughts in mind, I took a deep breath. "Thelma, I'm sorry to bother you, but I need help."

"Oh, my. This is awkward." Her smile faltered as her gaze went to my empty hands. "Usually when you need a favor, you bring me a treat. Something from Let's Bake a Deal. I thought we had an understanding."

"I'm sorry, Thelma."

With a sudden gasp, she leaned forward. "Patti didn't tell you I'm watching my weight, did she? That old gossip. I only told her that so she'd stop trying to get me to eat her pumpkin pie. It was way past its prime—and between you and me, I don't think she makes it fresh on the premises."

Patti ran the one and only restaurant in town—Patti's Diner. If residents wanted to eat anywhere else, we had to either drive west to Willow Falls or head south to Saratoga. The food at Patti's tasted okay, but as a college student working part-time, I rarely spent the money to eat out. Kevin's Kitchen, that was my hot spot.

Thelma continued prattling, to my utter fascination. How did a person talk without pausing for breath? I could stand and listen to her all day, usually. Not now, though.

"Sorry to interrupt, but it's an emergency. Can I come in? It's actually about Tony."

She took a step backward and held the door open. "Surely he's not too sick to bake."

I cleared my throat as I followed her down the hall into the living room. From experience, I knew she'd have a kettle on the stove and wouldn't want to answer my questions until we'd sat down and sipped our tea.

Sure enough, she walked straight into the kitchen, calling back over her shoulder for me to take a seat. There really didn't seem to be time to enjoy a refreshing beverage, but if Thelma didn't know the police were looking for me, it must not be common knowledge yet.

Usually I perched on the edge of her pink velvet settee and tried to finish the conversation as quickly as possible. Usually, I hadn't been living the same day on repeat. Sinking down onto the velvet, I leaned my head back against the top and closed my eyes.

"Now, what is the meaning of this?" Thelma asked, handing me a pink china teacup with a picture of her face on it and matching saucer. "What's going on with Tony that's serious enough you can't visit the bakery on your way here?"

"That's what I'd like to know. Do you know anyone who might want to hurt him?" Mary said if I figured out what happened to Tony, I could save us all. It might not make sense, but it was all I had to work with.

Thelma tilted her head for a moment and brought one

hand to her lips, always the actress. Whether she actually needed to collect her thoughts, I'd never know.

"Patti doesn't like Tony. Hates that people skip her over-baked desserts to buy his treats instead. But deep down, I think she knows even his day-old discount goods are better than her store-bought. Why do you ask?"

In for a penny, in for a pound. While I didn't trust Thelma further than I could throw the Hubble Space Telescope, right now, she was my best hope. "I hate to be the one to break this news to you, but Tony's dead. The Shady Grove police think I killed him."

She laughed, a tinkling high sound that reminded me of wind chimes. "Oh, my dear Aluminum, don't be ridiculous."

I blinked at her. "You don't believe me?"

"What is there to believe? Tony's not dead."

"I know it's hard to hear, but Sheriff Matthews found him a couple of hours ago."

She laughed. "What is today's date? It's a little early for April Fool's Day."

If I'd stopped to think about Thelma's reaction to learning that Tony was dead, absolute denial would not have been my first guess. Theatrics was her go-to trick. But also, this was weird. Thelma had known Tony for at least forty years. She must have. It was a small town, and she'd been visiting since childhood.

"I swear, I'm not joking, Thelma." I raised my right hand over my heart. "The police showed up at my house and told me that Tony died. They think I had something to do with it."

She snorted. "I always said that Sheriff Matthews was daft. As if you could hurt Tony. He's as strong as an ox."

An excellent point, under ordinary circumstances. "I'll tell them that when they show up to arrest me."

"Nonsense. Someone is pulling your leg. It must be your friend Rusty playing a trick on you." Before I could point out that Rusty was neither cruel nor callous, she continued.

"Tony's alive and well. He's on his way to his sister's wedding, where he'll be making the cake. Honestly, don't you pay any attention to what's happening in this town?"

My face grew warm. Since moving to Shady Grove, I'd been focused first on helping Kevin grieve, then on raising Kyle and solving Katrina's murder. More recently, my time had been largely occupied with classes, being psychic, and constantly finding myself embroiled in crime. So, no, I didn't pay a lot of attention to the daily lives of the town's other residents.

"Doug and Sheriff Matthews seem very convinced he is dead. Even if Rusty would make up a joke like that, it's hard to believe the sheriff would go along with it."

She rolled her eyes. "That sheriff is useless. You can practically see the mayor with her arm up his back, making his mouth move."

"Are you absolutely sure Tony is alive? When was the last time you talked to him?"

"Yes, I'm sure. I was just on the phone with Donna not ten minutes ago. She said she had to go because Tony had just arrived and she needed to talk to him about the dessert table for tomorrow's luncheon. I'm invited, you know. Planning to head up there after my shows."

Woo-hoo! I resisted the urge to shout with joy. Finally, some progress. Tony was alive, Thelma knew where he was, and I could get this mess sorted out before dinner.

"Do you know where the wedding is being held?" I asked.

"Certainly. Wait here. I've got the invitation on my fridge."

I would have expected Thelma to use something more glamorous than her fridge to keep track of social engagements, but it didn't surprise me that she'd been invited to the wedding. She was, after all, a fixture around here. She livened up any gathering. Besides, she'd trash you to everyone if she got left out.

"Ah, here it is."

Thelma returned from the kitchen and handed me a thickly embossed card. Donna Santoro and Alan Frazinetti, getting married tomorrow…a ha! And the location. Frazinetti's Lodge. Must be a family-owned place. But more importantly, the venue was located at the base of the mountains north of town. Still in Shady Grove County. I could be there in about half an hour.

Why the police couldn't figure this out was beyond me. They'd resolve crimes much faster if they knocked on Thelma's door once in a while.

Hold on. It was too early to celebrate.

When he went to the bakery, Jeff saw a chalk outline. Was that part of Mary's spell? Is that what she meant when she said *everyone* could be saved if I figured out what happened?

"Thank you so much, Thelma," I said. "Is it okay if I take a picture of this on my phone?"

"You can't *go to the wedding*, dear. Not if you weren't invited. Unless… do you know Alan? Are you in love with the groom? Oh, this is absolutely perfect." She clapped her hands in delight before leaning back and gazing at me sharply. "He is a little old for you, though, isn't he? I mean, he's nearly fifty. I thought you were with Olive's boy."

Rather than spoiling her one-woman show, I pulled out my phone to snap a picture of the info. That reminded me of the photo I'd taken earlier—Olive standing outside Tony's house. As suspected, it wasn't in my camera roll. This image wouldn't be enough if time reset. I needed to commit the address to memory and be on my way.

Time to down the rest of my tea for fortification, make a quick trip to the restroom, and I'd be on the road faster than you could say, "1.21 gigawatts."

The tea was delicious, warm, but not too hot. It traveled down smoothly, exactly what I needed after the stress of the past several hours. Or the past multiple reoccurrences of the same hour.

Suddenly, fists pounded on the front door. They'd found me! I jumped to my feet. My teacup crashed to the pink carpet. It shattered at my feet.

My eyes darted around frantically. Through the kitchen window, Doug walked from the front of the house toward the back stoop. "Thelma?"

"Oh, it's nothing to worry about, dear," she said calmly. "I expect that's the sheriff coming to take you away."

"Take me away? You said Tony's alive!"

"Yes, I did. All of that is true. But our illustrious police officers are looking for you, and I'm a law-abiding citizen. That Ellie next door is a huge gossip. I can't have her telling people I was harboring a *criminal* in my home. Just imagine what the town would say!"

My mouth dropped. "Is this because I didn't bring you cupcakes?"

"Don't be ridiculous, dear."

"Okay. So you're getting me arrested for something I didn't do to protect your reputation?"

"I don't *know* you didn't do it. After all, I suppose you might have murdered Tony right after I spoke with Donna, then driven down here to chat about it. But if you didn't, I have faith that you will clear it all up soon enough. You're a smart girl." She moved toward the front door. "Thank you for stopping by. It's always a pleasure."

Doug reached me before the sheriff, a minor blessing. At least he would be gentle.

I couldn't believe Thelma. No wonder she hadn't asked me more questions about Tony's supposed murder. She'd been just babbling to keep me occupied until the police showed up to haul me away.

The handcuffs clicked shut around my wrists while Doug recited the rights I'd heard a million times on TV. I didn't pay any attention to them. I wasn't talking. Chances were I wouldn't even make it to the police car.

Sheriff Matthews gloated from the doorway. If I hadn't already unleashed all my righteous fury on him once today, he might have been in for an earful. Instead I occupied myself by repeating the address on that invitation over and over. If Tony was there, I needed to find him ASAP.

"I can't believe you turned me in," I said as Doug led me past Thelma. "I thought we were friends. Or at least allies."

"Oh, Aluminum. You silly girl, you." As the door closed behind me, her carefully cultured voice carried clearly to my ears. "To think you told Julie Capaldi I can't act. Who looks foolish now?"

CHAPTER TWENTY-ONE

THE PACKAGE LOOKED COMPLETELY NORMAL. U.S. Priority Mail medium-sized box, just like my mom used whenever mailing us gifts. The stupid, cursed package that started this stupid, cursed day with its stupid, smelly chef's hat inside.

Thelma's betrayal stung, but it felt worse knowing I'd hurt her feelings. There wasn't much time to figure out what made her think I'd called her a bad actress. I didn't have to wonder how she found out—that women knew everything. But if I ever got out of this time loop, I swore to make things up to her. If Tony turned out to be alive, I could bring her those cupcakes she loved so much.

For now, I raced to my car once again. If Tony was at some lodge preparing for his sister's wedding, I needed to be there.

Thus far, all of my efforts to leave Shady Grove had been unsuccessful. I couldn't get to Willow Falls. But the lodge sat at the edge of Shady Grove County. How big was this spell? I was about to find out.

I didn't have any better ideas, so I prayed this would work.

As quickly yet safely as I could manage, I put the house

behind me and turned toward the road that would lead me to I-87 and out of town. The resort listed on the invitation had been unfamiliar, but I remembered the address well enough to speak it into my GPS.

Although I expected the effort to be futile, I asked my phone to call Kevin again while I drove. Nothing. I also requested a text that said "Emergency. Call immediately." It failed. What else could I do?

Something had been nagging at the back of my mind for a while now. Finally, it hit me: when Olive and I had gone to Tony's house, we found the realtor lying dead at the bottom of a collapsed staircase. When had he arrived? Amira had planned to go to a showing at four; we'd gotten there around three-thirty. What if Todd had died shortly before we found him?

I hadn't checked his pulse, hadn't felt his body. Olive swore his head was lying at such an unnatural angle that he couldn't possibly have survived the fall. But what if he'd been only very recently dead?

More importantly, what if he had been traveling to Tony's house when I got to Missing Pieces, and I could avoid his death by skipping the store and getting there first? Maybe I could stop him from entering the basement and dying on the staircase.

It might be a wild goose chase. But I didn't have anything to lose by heading over there, and maybe I could save Todd.

Maybe I was *meant* to save Todd.

Maybe this entire terrible day was all about me saving Todd, and I could end the time loop by getting to Tony's house in time.

That made no sense at all. Why would Mary care if Todd died? For that matter, why would Mary care about saving Tony? But at this point, I had a huge problem to solve, a lot of half-formed hypotheses, and it all came back down to this:

Mary was messing with me to get to Kyle, and she didn't care who she hurt along the way.

It was worth a try. There was nothing to lose. If I got there and Todd was dead, I could go to the wedding. Or I could go back to Thelma's house. I'd forgotten to ask if she knew the realtor.

A few minutes later, I arrived on Tony's street. This time, when I pulled up in front of the "For Sale" sign, I examined the surrounding area more carefully. If I remembered correctly, Todd worked in Willow Falls. While I supposed he might live around here, more likely, he'd driven. So where was his car? No one but me was parked in front of the house. I spotted a couple of vehicles further down the street, but it seemed silly to park a block away when preparing to show a house.

Had I spotted a car when Olive and I came by before? I racked my brain, but I just couldn't remember. Nor did I have any idea what kind of car Todd drove.

New question: was Todd meeting with a buyer? Maybe he'd had an appointment with someone who pushed him down the stairs. If I went into the basement and unlocked his phone, it might give me a clue what happened.

The two-family home contained a two-car garage. The door was closed, but if Tony and Donna were both away for the day, maybe Todd had pulled inside.

Trying my best to look unsuspicious and not at all like someone breaking and entering, I walked up the driveway. There was a side door, but with white blinds pulled over the window, I couldn't see anything. Time to go inside.

This time, when I got to the front porch, the doors were locked. Both of them. Maybe I'd done it! I'd gotten here before Todd! This was my chance to save him.

Of course, now I needed to get inside. I checked under the doormat for a key and found nothing. Then I spotted the lockbox hanging off the railing.

One of the more useful things I'd learned from my powers was how to call visions of people entering information onto keypads. It didn't always work—and in fact, probably wouldn't have, if I hadn't met the realtor last year. Good thing Shady Grove and Willow Falls shared a real estate firm.

Closing my eyes, I conjured a memory of my one and only meeting with Todd Lacroix. Shiny blond hair with a middle part he could have drawn with a ruler. Straight white teeth. Very nice suit. I could see why Amira would be interested. He hadn't been terribly nice to me, but then again, he'd thought I was a burglar.

Holding that memory firmly in my mind, I reached for the lockbox and entered four zeroes.

I didn't expect 0000 to be the code, and it wasn't. As I attempted to use the lockbox while remembering Todd, I saw a pair of perfectly manicured hands holding the box. Not mine—the nails were wider, the fingers longer. While I watched, Todd punched four numbers into the lockbox. Perfect.

"Thanks, Todd," I muttered as I opened my eyes and repeated the gesture. The box popped open, revealing two house keys. One for each door, presumably. I took them both.

A loud honk made me jump. A shiny white BMW screeched to a stop in the driveway, the driver laying on the horn.

My heart pounded. This car didn't have any salt on it, even though the roads were covered with snow. It must be recently washed. A memory flashed through my mind. The same vehicle had been across the street when Olive and I showed up earlier.

The driver's side door flew open. A man jumped out just as I realized who it must be.

I choked. Todd LaCroix stood in Tony's driveway, very much alive.

"Hey! You! What are you doing to my lockbox?"

A huge peal of laughter escaped me. I dropped the lockbox and pumped my fist in the air. "Yes! Oh my goodness. I'm so glad to see you!"

Todd had been storming up the driveway toward me, but suddenly he stopped in his tracks. He raised both hands in the universal "stop" sign. "Hey, sorry. Everything is fine. Nothing to see here. I'm just going to get back in my car. Hold on. Do I know you?"

Great. Now this guy thought I was a criminal. After I came here to save him!

Okay, Aly. Act normal.

I forced myself to calm down and smile, trying to look non-threatening. "Hi, Todd. My name is Aly Reynolds. We met a few months ago. At a house you were selling in Willow Falls."

His eyes narrowed. "Yes, we did. I remember now. You'd broken into that property. And here you are again. What is wrong with you?"

Oh, fluorine. This wasn't going at all like I'd planned.

"Oh, no. I wasn't breaking in. I stopped by to see if Tony is okay. He's a friend of mine, and I heard something was wrong. I was worried."

"A friend of yours who you couldn't have called before dropping by? Because if you had, you'd know I'm doing showings all day. The owner can't be around for that."

I shuddered to think what would have happened if his first clients had arrived to find Todd lying at the bottom of a fallen staircase with a broken neck. Good thing I'd made it in time.

"Okay, okay. You've got me. The truth is, you can't go in there. The house isn't safe. There's a huge structural problem with the staircase. It's going to collapse when you put your weight on it."

Todd nodded slowly. "Oh, yeah? Great! Thank you so much for letting me know. Tell you what. Let me call a building inspector. We'll sit out on the stoop and wait for him."

Yeah, right. The "building inspector" would probably arrive with a straitjacket.

"I know how this looks, but you've got to believe me. You can't go in there."

Sirens screamed in the distance.

Uh-oh. A coincidence? Unlikely. Luck hadn't been exactly on my side today.

Todd must have called them when he was pulling up. Considering we were at Tony's house, it wouldn't have taken the police long to figure out the identity of the twenty-one-year-old medium-height brunette breaking in.

Time to go.

Even though he was getting me arrested, I had to make one last effort to save this man's life. I moved toward my car. "Listen, Todd, I know you think I'm some kind of house-breaking weirdo, but I'm right about this. Do not go into that house. It's not safe."

A police car exploded around the corner. Couldn't go that way. No time to get into my car. I did the next best thing: running as fast as I could. Another police car turned onto the road ahead, leaving me blocked between the two.

Veering left, I sprinted across the nearest lawn and bolted through a fence. Or as close to sprinting as a person can do through six inches of snow. The police probably saw me, but I had a head start. As long as they didn't shoot, I might have a chance.

Furious barking brought me to a screeching halt. I stopped so fast, my foot skidded on the ice. I went flying. My butt hit the ground with a painful thud. A pit bull sprang into view, racing toward me. Who knew this would be the end?

Hold on. That dog looked very familiar. Didn't I know someone with a pit bull? Yes! Wendy Diaz, one of the bowlers in Kevin's league, had mentioned him when I met her almost a year ago.

"Fluffykins?"

The dog stopped.

"Gooooooood Fluffykins."

He cocked his head, lifting one ear toward me. Then he whined, pawing at the ground. What had Wendy said about this dog? He was scared of his own shadow.

Something over the past several months must have given Fluffykins some self-confidence, because he was putting on a good show of planning to rip my throat out if I moved.

Then Doug's face appeared over the back fence, and the dog didn't matter anymore.

"Give it up, Aly. It's over."

I sighed. Yes, it was.

Goodbye, Fluffykins. Time to rewind.

CHAPTER TWENTY-TWO

THE PACKAGE. That stupid package. I grabbed it and raced for my car while trying to figure out how to stop Todd from entering Tony's house and getting killed. Or calling the police on me. Did I need to stop him from going into the house forever, or just temporarily? I could pretend to want to make an offer on one of his other listings far, far away and ask him to meet me there.

While I drove, I asked my phone to dial.

"Todd LaCroix."

"Hi, Todd, my name is Aly Reynolds. I'm looking to buy a house, and I heard that you have the most amazing place for sale." I cast my mind around desperately. "A two-bedroom?"

"Willow Falls or Shady Grove?"

"Willow Falls!" That was nowhere near Tony's house. The perfect place to stop Todd from getting killed. He wouldn't know I couldn't actually go there without bouncing back to my brother's house like a repelled electron.

"I've got several listings. Can you tell me more about what you're looking for?"

"Um, I love a screened-in porch…?" There must be something like that around here somewhere.

"Oh, yes! The place on Riverdale. How did you even know about it? The listing just went live."

"Um, the owner works with a friend of mine."

"The owners are retired," he said skeptically.

"I mean, before they retired. Anyway, can you meet me to hash out an offer immediately?"

"You don't want to see it?"

"Oh, it's okay. I've been there before. It's exactly what I want. Are you free now? Now is a really good time for me." The urgency in my voice was palpable. I needed to rein it in, or I'd freak this guy out.

"You know, I love your tenacity. You've got great energy." He was quiet for a moment. "I'm sorry, but I can't meet you now. I'm doing showings in Shady Grove all evening. Are you free tomorrow morning?"

"No!" The word slipped out. "I mean, it needs to be right now."

"You have to meet with me immediately or not at all?"

"Yes? I'm, um, late for the airport." It sounded weak even to me. Really, I should have scripted this better, but I didn't have a lot of time. Or, I had all the time in the world, depending on how you looked at it.

"I guess this is goodbye then," Todd said. "I'm a man of my word, and I can't cancel my appointments."

Before I could protest further, he hung up on me.

Great. Now how was I supposed to keep him from going inside Tony's house? I could—burn it down? Maybe Amira's "ghost" would come with me.

No.

Call 911 and report a gas leak?

That would just hurt whoever investigated. I wasn't going to save Todd at the expense of someone else.

Now that I thought about it—how did Mary even know Todd? Why was she trying to save him? Yes, he'd been selling "her" house when we'd met, but our discussion at the time had left me convinced Mary didn't actually own the place and had just been using the empty home to meet with me.

The drive to Tony's took ages now that I knew a man's life hung in the balance. But I'd witnessed enough horrible accidents today. I wasn't about to take my chances getting into another one.

To my immense relief, Tony's driveway was still empty when I arrived at the house. The time on my phone said Todd would be here in a few minutes if my memory could be trusted. At this point, who knew?

Okay, minutes. What to do?

Maybe I could make the house safe. Last time, Todd pulled up while I was opening the lockbox. I'd wasted time trying to break into the garage, but still. I needed to move fast. Instead of making myself so visible, I reached casually over the back fence and lifted the latch before sliding the wood open.

An untouched layer of snow blanketed the backyard. Someone had cleared the back porch, though. Todd probably worked hard to ensure everything was perfect.

He wouldn't like if it something messed that up. Hmm. Did Fluffykins like to dig? Could I lure Wendy's dog over here somehow?

To do what, exactly?

Too late. Todd's car was pulling into the driveway. I darted through a rear door of the house. Yay for small towns and trusting residents who never locked their doors. Now I stood in Tony's kitchen, mere inches from the basement. I wondered if I could make it down the stairs before getting caught.

Todd was several inches taller than me and fairly muscular. He probably outweighed me by close to forty pounds. I was a relatively small person, but I also wasn't feeling lucky enough to stand on rotted wood and hope it held.

At least I could open the door and look. Maybe there was something obviously wrong I could fix.

You know, with all those carpentry skills I picked up working at the antique store.

With no better plan, I opened the door to the shared basement and flipped on the light switch. From here, the stairs looked perfectly normal. Leaning over, I shook the banister. It barely moved.

Nope. This was never going to work. I needed to get out of here and call a building inspector.

"What are you doing here?"

Whirling around, I found myself face-to-face with Todd LaCroix. I grabbed at the first excuse I could think of. "Amira told me you're doing showings all day today. I thought there might be an open house."

"Yeah, there is. But it doesn't start for a couple of hours. Also, the front door was locked. You shouldn't be here." He peered closely at me. "Do I know you?"

"I don't think so," I said. "But a lot of people think I look like Anna Kendrick."

"Who?"

"The actress in Pitch Perfect." He gave me a blank look, so I kept talking. Anything to keep him from either dying or calling the police. "I've been told I have one of those faces. Listen, this is a gorgeous house. Are you selling both units or the whole thing together?"

"The sellers would prefer to sell the entire property to one buyer. But it's great for renting out the other side, getting an investment income going. What's your price range?"

Currently, I paid zero dollars per month in rent, which was absolutely within my budget. Instead of telling him that, I said, "Oh, I'm looking for my brother. He's a lawyer."

"You're Kevin Reynolds's sister?"

Oops. I forgot everyone around here knows everyone else. "Guilty. You know Kevin?"

"I helped him find a new house after his wife died. Now that's a sweet property." He paused. "Sorry about your sister-in-law."

"Thanks. Listen, this banister doesn't look right. I really think you should cancel the showings and get it checked out."

"What?"

"This house isn't safe," I repeated. "You can't go into the basement. You could get seriously hurt."

He scoffed. "That's ridiculous. Tony and I went through the entire house last week. He fixed the whole thing up himself, did you know that? The man's an artist."

Considering how beautiful his cakes looked, that wasn't a complete surprise. But if Tony redid everything, how did the basement stairs crumble?

Moving past me, Todd stepped down onto the wooden steps.

"Stop!" I squeaked out.

"Really, it's fine. I know some people find basements to be scary, but this one has been completely finished from top to bottom." He kept talking as he moved further down the stairs. Words like "baseboards" and other nonsense.

"Please stop!" I said. "I can't explain it, but I have a very bad feeling about this."

Halfway down, he finally paused. "You're being ridiculous. Look. Everything is solid."

To prove his point, Todd jumped in place.

The wooden stair cracked, then buckled. Todd lunged for the banister. It swung wildly away from the wall. He flailed. I raced to his aid.

And the two of us crashed to the newly installed polished concrete floor.

My head slammed into the ground. The world swam around me. Everything turned gray.

CHAPTER TWENTY-THREE

THE PACKAGE LOOKED COMPLETELY NORMAL. U.S. Priority Mail medium-sized box, just like my mom used whenever mailing us gifts. Just like I'd seen six hundred times today already. Always at two-fifty-seven. My least favorite time.

Okay, I could do this. Deep breaths.

Element one was hydrogen. Element two was helium. Element three was lithium.

At least now I had a purpose. Grab the keys, get in the car, go to Tony's house. Call Amira, tell her to shut off the breakers in the magic store and call an electrician. Also to cancel her showing, because it wasn't happening. My friend didn't need to worry about finding or becoming a dead body. Text Tiffaneigh to have her brakes checked. Tell Todd the building inspector had found mold and the showings all needed to be rescheduled. Call Sam. Check, check, check, check.

Now what? Over the past several hours, I'd turned to almost everyone I knew for help finding out who killed Tony. Then Thelma told me Tony was alive. Maybe all I needed to do was convince Sheriff Matthews? Today hadn't exactly been going my way, but it might help to have a lawyer on my side.

Kevin couldn't do anything, obviously, and he was the only practicing attorney in Shady Grove. There was, however, a former lawyer. One who happened to be dating my brother. This time, after I got in my car and started the engine, I told my phone to call Julie.

The display showed a pretty blue-eyed blonde laughing up at me. Her arms were thrown around my brother, who was bending her over backward in an exaggerated dip. It was one of my favorite pictures of them, taken shortly after their team won some bowling competition. Kevin had been so closed down ever since Katrina died. I loved seeing him find his old sense of fun now that he and Julie were together.

She answered on the third ring. "On What Grounds?. This is Julie. How can I help you?"

I heaved a sigh of relief. "Thank goodness you answered. I need help."

Concern filled her voice. I could almost see her brow furrowing as she registered my words. "Aly?"

"Yeah. Listen, it's hard to explain, but I need a lawyer."

"Hold on a sec. I need to move to the back room." The line went silent but not dead. On What Grounds? didn't have hold music.

An eternity passed before she picked up again. I'd started to think Julie was going to leave me hanging. But she was a good person. She loved Kevin and adored Kyle. We'd been becoming friends even before she started dating my brother. Now, I considered her family. With any luck, one day, she would be.

"You know I'm not a lawyer anymore, right?"

"I know you don't practice. But... I also may or may not know that there is still an active law license under the name of Julie Capaldi."

She swore under her breath. "I'm going to kill Rusty."

"It's not his fault. He can't resist showing off his PI skills."

"Some skills," she grumbled. "What did he do, type my name into the state bar's website?"

"Yes, in fact, he did, but that's not the point. Listen. I need help." Still driving in circles, I explained my situation while keeping an eye out for police cars. This wasn't exactly safe, but being in motion made me feel better than sitting still. "Tony's not dead. I need someone to go to the police station with me and tell them."

"You know you didn't kill Tony," she said. "The police seem pretty sure he's dead. Have you confirmed whether he is alive?"

"No, but Thelma said—"

"Thelma will say absolutely anything to get attention," Julie reminded me. "And she can't even confirm telling you that because, if I understand you correctly, it didn't happen in this reality, right?"

"No, it didn't. Oh! Did you tell her I said she can't act?"

"Aly! Is that really important at the moment?"

"Considering she used it as a reason to sell me out to the police, I'm going with yes."

"I never said a word. I don't even remember you saying that," Julie said. "But remember, we were watching *As the Hospital Guides Our Lives* at the coffee shop with Amber last week?"

Since Rusty left the coffee shop to pursue a full-time job as a private investigator, a parade of baristas had been in and out. Amber was one of the newer ones, a high school student who seemed great but could only work nights and weekends. "No? I mean, we watch that a lot."

"I'd just made a fresh batch of blueberry peach muffins."

"Oh! Of course!" Names and faces may elude me, but I never forgot a truly excellent baked good. "I never said Thelma couldn't act. I was complaining that everyone on the show spoke like they were chewing—oh. How does Amber even know Thelma?"

"A, Thelma knows everyone. B, Amber is one of Ellie's granddaughters. Do you want me to tell Amber you didn't mean it?"

I thought for a minute. "It's too late now. If I have another time loop, she won't remember. I'll apologize to Thelma next time I see her. In any reality I should find myself in."

"You just need proof Tony is alive, right?"

"I think so."

"Great. I can help with that. I'll meet you, and we'll get proof together. Are you someplace safe?"

I glanced out my car's window, into the depths of the Nature Preserve bordering Maloney College. It seemed like as good a place to go as any when the police were looking for you. Except, if I tried to lose myself in the trees, the fresh snow would out me. "Yeah, I guess. Why?"

"Sheriff Matthews and Doug are at Missing Pieces now, talking to Olive. I can go over there and intervene on your behalf. They can't make me tell them where you are."

"You don't know where I am."

"Exactly. Let me feel them out and then call you back. When I do, I'm going to use a code word so you know they're not listening. Okay?"

"Sure," I said. "Can it be Kelvin?"

My brother's legal name would never stop being a source of amusement to me. Mostly I only needled him when he was around to hear about it, but Julie would surely pass that tidbit on when she talked to him.

She chuckled. "Speaking of your brother, what does he have to say about all this?"

"I don't know," I admitted. "Mary blocked me from calling him after the time loop started."

"Sit tight. Let's see if I can call him."

"Thank you," I said. "I owe you."

"Don't be ridiculous," Julie replied. "We're practically sisters."

Time ticked by at an agonizingly slow speed while I waited for her to call me back. I didn't think for a second that she'd get Kevin on the phone, but maybe she could talk to Sheriff Matthews. She'd meet me at the police station, we would clear my name, Tony would appear and serve us all cake, this day would finally end, and tomorrow we could do the spell to find Mary and make sure she never, ever pulled a stunt like this again.

A beautiful plan.

Alas, not meant to be.

The display on my phone lit up with Julie's face a second time. Not that I was looking at it instead of the road. Immediately, I answered. "How did it go?"

"On a scale of one to ten, I'd say about a nine for me. More like a three for Julie," a deep voice responded. "How are you, Ms. Reynolds? We've been looking for you."

My mouth went paper dry. "Sheriff Matthews? What's going on?"

"Oh, nothing. I thought you'd like to know that your friend Ms. Capaldi has been arrested for aiding and abetting a fleeing felon. You know what the sentence on that is?"

Nearly twenty seconds passed before I found my voice. "She wasn't helping me. Julie's a lawyer."

"That's not how the jury will see it," he replied. "Ten years. She's looking at ten years, if I have anything to say about it. And when we find you, it'll be three times that."

"But I didn't do anything. Neither, by the way, did she."

"I'm sure you're both saints. By the way, we're tracing this call. Looks like I finally got a bead on you. See you in a minute, Ms. Reynolds."

My mind insisted he was bluffing. Stabbing the "end call" button on my console, I slammed the car into reverse and pushed on the accelerator. My car leapt back in a circle.

As I shifted into drive, flashing blue and red lights appeared on the road. I held my breath, praying they would continue past me. No such luck. Reaching out to Julie for help wasn't the way to clear my name and find Tony, after all.

Hello, mist. I embraced it.

CHAPTER TWENTY-FOUR

THE PACKAGE LOOKED COMPLETELY NORMAL. A standard U.S. Priority Mail medium-sized box, just like my mom used whenever mailing us gifts. Once again, my phone showed 2:57 on the display. Just once, I'd like it to be 2:56 or 2:58.

Deep breaths. I could do this. At least I wasn't under arrest.

Besides, I had a purpose now. Grab the keys, get in the car, go to Tony's house. Call Amira, tell her to shut off the breakers and call an electrician before her store catches fire. Text Tiffaneigh to have her brakes checked.

Drive to Tony's house. Tell Todd the building inspector had found mold and the open house needed to be rescheduled. Check, check, check.

I waited patiently while Todd made some calls to cancel showings before realizing that standing here wouldn't tell me whether I'd ended the loop. He wasn't going to die now (probably). Was that enough?

Pulling out my phone, I called Kevin. It went straight to voicemail. Slightly worrying, but inconclusive. Just in case, I left a message. Next, I called Mrs. Patel, with the same results.

Not terribly surprising, since she was with Kevin. On a whim, I tried my mom in Sacramento. Voicemail.

Now what?

If saving Todd was the task Mary set for me, I should be able to go home and pick up where I left off with the cookie dough and Mercury the Turtle. But then—why the chef's hat? What about the police? Saving Todd wouldn't magically undo those things, would it?

I could try again to go see Emma, but since she didn't answer her phone when I tapped her name, I had a sneaking suspicion that was not the answer. Maybe I needed to physically find and talk to Tony, after all. Just realizing he wasn't dead might not be enough.

After checking yet again to ensure that Todd wasn't about to enter the house and fall through a rotting staircase, I left.

First, I went to swap cars with Rusty for the second time. While my little Prius was likely safe once I got a couple of miles north and got better gas mileage, my best friend's SUV had all-wheel drive. The roads near the mountains could be a total mess this time of year. Before driving away, I reminded myself not to leave the orb in the trunk. If nothing else, I could chuck it at Mary's head should the opportunity arise. Hug Rusty goodbye. Set GPS coordinates for Frazinetti Lodges. Do not pass Go, do not collect $200. Text Sam to make sure he talks to me before leaving for Shady Grove in the morning and avoids all construction sites.

It took about fifteen tries, but finally, I was on my way to the lodge.

Hopefully. There was only one way to tell.

As Shady Grove moved into my rearview mirror, my entire body relaxed. I couldn't go east to find Kevin in Boston. I couldn't go west to ask Emma for help. But I could drive north and find Tony. Maybe I'd finally found the road out of this mess.

CHAPTER TWENTY-FIVE

ABOUT FIFTEEN MINUTES LATER, my GPS directed me to turn off the mostly clear highway onto the first of many less-than-stellar roads. My Prius wasn't built for off-roading, so I was very grateful for Rusty's SUV. Still, even with all-wheel drive, I slowed to a crawl. I'd had enough accidents today to last a lifetime.

By the time I pulled into the unpaved lot of a small mountain resort, the sun was setting, and I was starving. I couldn't remember the last time I'd eaten. The sign assured me that I'd reached Frazinetti Lodges. It also informed me the place was closed for a private event, so hopefully I could find Tony and convince him to go back to town with me before bedtime. Otherwise, I'd be sleeping in Rusty's back seat.

The path from the parking area led up a slight incline to what appeared to be the main rental office and a meeting area or down the hill a bit toward a stable. Through the large windows of the main office, I spotted people mingling around, drinking and eating appetizers. It must be cocktail hour. I absolutely wasn't dressed for it, and bluffing my way in would be hard enough even if the bride and groom weren't there to realize neither of them invited me. But I was almost hungry enough to try.

To get out of the cold, I headed inside the building. It was small, with six stalls, two of them empty. There was an attached pasture, but I hadn't seen any animals roaming around. A black horse stuck his face over the stall and nickered at me. After he sniffed my hand and lowered his head in consent, I stroked his nose.

"Hey, there. You don't happen to know where I can find Tony, do you?"

Not surprisingly, the horse didn't answer.

"Listen, I'm working on it!" I jumped, but the voice wasn't coming from the horse. It carried through a small window in the stall. A shadow passed as someone walked by the outdoor light, and I dropped to the floor before they spotted me. "You'll get your money!"

Money? Still in a crouch, I moved as quietly as possible to the empty stall beside the black horse and slunk my way inside. Hardly daring to breathe, I flattened myself under the window and prepared to listen.

A second man answered the first. This one had a higher voice, somewhat nasally. "You keep saying that, but it's been months. How do you plan to get the money before the end of the month?"

"I've got things in motion. They're just taking some time to pay off."

"Oh, yeah? Is this like your 'make a reality show set at the resort' plan? Because we both remember how that worked out for you."

"No! This is good! A sure thing. My brother-in-law, he runs this bakery. He's got some amazing stuff. He made the wedding cake, plus he's catering lunch tomorrow. Making these meat pies my girl loves. Come have a drink with me, and I'll show you how talented he is."

"No, thanks." The second man sounded remarkably unimpressed. "Is your talented future brother-in-law planning to pay off your mortgage?"

"He may not know it yet, but yes, he is. I've got a friend who owns a grocery store chain. He wants to add some fresh baked goods."

"How does that help you?"

"My bride, Donna, that's how. She works in the bakery. Once we're married, she's going to sign the deal and start cooking. We'll make money hand over fist. The store owner has already promised a very generous signing bonus. Everything is under control."

"Okay, then." Guy #2 spoke slowly, as if not entirely convinced. "Show me the contract when it's signed, and maybe I'll consider giving you more time. There's going to be interest, though. And you know I always collect my interest."

Terror filled the deeper voice when he replied. "Y-yes. I know. You'll get paid. I swear on my mother's grave."

"Oh, it's not going to be your mother's grave," the other person responded. "If you catch my meaning."

A chill went down my spine. For the first time, it occurred to me that eavesdropping may not be a good idea. Whoever was threatening Donna's fiancé probably wouldn't appreciate having a witness.

"I get you," the guy who must be Alan Frazinetti said. "I won't let you down. I promise."

"Wait here. I'll leave first."

A moment later, a car door slammed. An engine roared to life. Tires crackled on the gravel driveway, and then the car moved away.

I stayed in place, not wanting either of the men to find me. Then the second man moved in front of the window, and I held my breath while studying his profile.

Please, please don't look inside the stall.

Luck must've been on my side. Not only did he not glance through the stable window, but now I knew Donna's fiancé was medium height with dark hair and a long, thin scar down the left side of his face. Also, he owed someone a lot of money and was hoping to get it from Tony.

People had killed for less.

After a moment, a second set of footsteps trailed away from me. Finally, I could breathe again—but I couldn't move on yet. The path between here and the main lodge was long and open. Even in the waning light, I'd be seen if I went out before Alan made it up the hill and inside.

After reciting every element of the periodic table, I felt safe enough to leave my hiding spot. With a deep breath, I crawled back toward the stall door. Then I realized how silly I must look and moved to stand upright. After wiping my dirty palms on my yoga pants, I stepped back into the main hallway. The friendly horse returned to nuzzle my neck.

I patted his nose a second time. "Thanks for not giving me away. Sorry I don't have any carrots."

Bracing myself against the cold, I left the relative safety of the stable. This conversation had given me a very important piece of information. Alan needed money. If she sold her home, Donna would have money. To me, that seemed to suggest she wouldn't have killed her realtor. Not that I thought she did, but she was one of a few people with access to that basement.

Skirting around the windows, I examined the area. A wooden sign with arrows pointed out the cabins, the stable, and the main lodge. Tony presumably had rented a cabin somewhere in the woods, but wandering around aimlessly made no sense.

A smaller building was attached to the largest cabin by a brick tunnel. Smoke rose from a chimney attached to the side of that building. It must be the kitchen. If Tony was providing food for the wedding, that would be the logical place to find him. Assuming Thelma had been right, and he was still alive.

Crunching my way through the snow, I found the rear door. With my hand on the handle, I hesitated.

Now what?

Did I just march in? "Hey, man! I know you weren't expecting to see me here since we're essentially strangers, but are you by any chance dead?"

I shook my head. Step one: verify that Tony is alive. Step two: convince the Shady Grove Sheriff's Department. That should break the time loop and get me to tomorrow. Step three: stop Mary from ever doing something like this again.

The back door swung open easily at my touch. When no one appeared to ask what I was doing there, I took a tentative step inside. The kitchen was empty. No chef walking around barking orders. No food waiting to be served. No waitstaff wandering in and out.

Either the cocktail hour had been catered, or the food had been finished quite a while ago. Only a couple of dishes in the sink and a row of mixing bowls on the counter against the far wall gave any proof of life.

I moved toward a swinging door in the same direction as the main lodge and put my eye to the window. Nothing but the tunnel I'd seen from outside. It must've been added to allow servers to take food to and from the larger building in the snow.

Glancing down at my yoga pants—which now had straw sticking to them in two places—I opted not to crash the fancy party. I didn't have any other clothes in my trunk.

Note to self: keep clothes in your trunk, just in case. And in Rusty's trunk.

The walk-in fridge and freezer were stocked, but empty of people. No wedding cake, either. Huh.

Curious, I approached the counter. If the chef had been in the middle of something before getting called away, maybe he'd be back soon. White powder covered the stainless steel surface. Each bowl contained a couple of balls of dough.

Reaching out a hand, I touched the metal. Still cool from the fridge. A bag of flour sat near the wall next to a rolling pin. After my conversation with Tiffaneigh, I felt silly for not realizing what it was in my vision.

Leaning forward, I picked up the pin, savoring the feel of the cool wood in my palms. I wasn't much of a baker, but when I was a kid, I loved rolling out sugar cookies with my mom. Lost in the memory, I closed my eyes and moved the pin across the countertop.

All of a sudden, an image swam before my eyes. Not a memory of making sugar cookies with my mom, but a vision.

Empty baking sheets lined one wall. The dough in front of me was no longer in bowls but rolled out in two large rectangles. From what little I could see, this appeared to be the same kitchen. Behind me, someone was talking in a low, gravelly voice.

"Come on, Tony, this is a great deal!"

I grunted and didn't respond.

"Don't you want your sister to be happy?"

"My sister was perfectly happy working with me in the bakery and living under the same roof. She doesn't need you to take her away."

"I'm not taking her away. I'm expanding her horizons. And if you would stop being such a grouch for three seconds, you'd be happy for us."

"I'm not gonna be happy for some smooth-talking greaseball coming in and filling my sister's head with lies."

Tony must be talking to Donna's fiancé, Alan. This conversation mirrored the one I'd overheard in the stable.

Earlier, Alan had made it sound like Tony was helping him with his plan to sell the cupcakes. What if—

Someone grabbed me from behind. I gasped. A meaty hand clamped over my mouth.

Tony! He'd killed his realtor, and now he planned to kill me!

Without thinking, acting purely on instinct, I employed

the self-defense moves Maria had taught me. Stomp on the instep.

He grunted.

I slammed my elbow back into his solar plexus. He loosened his grip. Grabbing the rolling pin from the counter, I swung to my side, trying to get my assailant to back off.

It worked!

I spun around, still brandishing the rolling pin.

In the dim light, a man stood doubled over, still wheezing.

"Oh. No. You don't." He gasped out. "You're not getting my recipes."

The man looked at me, and I nearly screamed. Tony.

Then he charged. I lifted the rolling pin.

All of a sudden, I understood the vision from the baker's hat.

CHAPTER TWENTY-SIX

NOPE, not like this. No matter what happened in that vision, Mary wasn't going to get me. I refused to kill Tony. Not even in self-defense. Even if I put aside all the other reasons, I desperately didn't want to loop again. Killing Tony seemed like a great way to put me back in Kevin's foyer, holding that stupid package.

Tony charged. I stepped out of the way, hurrying to put a counter between us. He slammed into it, knocking the wind out of himself.

Before he could do anything, I spoke quickly. "Tony, stop! It's me, Aly."

"Who?"

"Aly Reynolds. From Shady Grove. My brother's the lawyer."

"Tin Foil Girl?" He looked me up and down and nodded, more to himself than me. "What are you doing here?"

My hands went straight to my hips as I pulled myself to my full height in righteous indignation. "You call me *Tin Foil Girl*?"

He snorted. "Don't tell me you haven't heard it before."

"Of course I have. I expected you to be more original." We

were getting off track. "Let's start over. Hi! I'm here because the Shady Grove police think you're dead, and someone told them I killed you."

"You?" He pushed away from the counter and stood upright, rubbing his head. "Why would you want to kill me?"

"I don't. You attacked me just now," I said. "I was trying to protect myself. It's okay, though. You're alive. I'm unharmed. Everything's peachy. Let's go back to Shady Grove, you can explain you're not dead, and the police will stop trying to arrest me. It's a quick drive. If we leave now, you'll be back before it's time to serve dessert. Everyone wins!"

"Why would I do that for you?"

The question stopped me in my tracks. It never occurred to me that Tony wouldn't want people to know he wasn't dead. "Um… because your friends and family will be sad if you're dead? The town is probably going to host a funeral. You know Thelma never misses an opportunity to sing."

He chuckled. "I can see why you'd want to cancel that. But look at me, I'm busy. I can't leave my sister's wedding."

Tony flipped a switch, and the lights came on. We were standing in a kitchen, as I'd known, but what I hadn't realized was that Tony had already completed several batches of baked goods. A baker's rack against the wall appeared to be filled with tray after tray of mouth-watering delicacies.

"What's going on here? You faked your death and left town to do a catering job?" Even to my own ears, that sounded completely ridiculous.

"Don't be dumb," Tony said. "I didn't fake my death. I'm here to do the dessert table for my sister's wedding. And I'm way behind because some annoying girl was on her phone in my bakery instead of ordering so I could get on the road on time."

"You could—" I stopped and clenched my teeth. "If you didn't fake your death, why do the cops think I killed you?"

"Nu-uh. That's enough chitchat. You want to talk, put on an apron. I could use the extra hands."

When I protested, he crossed his arms over his chest and mimicked zipping his lips. Wonderful.

I glanced at the sky. "Ready to reset me? I could use a good time loop."

Nothing happened.

Tony shook his head. "Kids today. I'll never get all your jokes and your fancy technology."

Technology! Before I wasted time baking—something which was not my forte and never had been, although I could follow directions—I needed to make a call.

"Hold on, Tony," I said. "I will help you, but I need to talk to Doug first. Let him know that you're alive."

"Good luck. There's no cell service up here."

"Don't you have a landline?"

"Sure I do." Walking over to the wall, Tony unplugged the receiver and put it in his pocket. "Thanks for reminding me. Now grab an apron."

Really, I should've seen that coming. With a sigh, I followed Tony's pointing finger to several clean aprons hanging on a hook on the wall. I grabbed a hot pink one, hoping the bright color would lift my mood.

Not quite ready to give up, when I pulled it over my head, I slipped my phone out of my pocket and checked the home screen.

No bars. Darn it. Tony was right. My only way out of this was to help him. At least until I found another phone.

When I turned back around, a rubber band bounced off my nose. "Pull your hair back."

I tried to remember if my vision had shown my hair pulled back. Maybe the scene where I murdered Tony hadn't occurred yet, and this entire situation was all about mounting my provocation argument.

"Don't just stand there. Make yourself useful. Turn the ovens to 350."

Shaking those thoughts away, I moved toward the wall and pressed some buttons. After my last experience with a gas stove, I was relieved to see these were electric. Then I turned back toward Tony, hands on my hips. "Is this a good time to mention I don't know how to bake?"

"Then there's no time like the present to learn." He went to the fridge and pulled out two mixing bowls. "You got a kid, right?"

"My nephew, Kyle. Why?" Although only four, Kyle was significantly better in the kitchen than I. He liked to watch cooking and baking shows on Netflix and then order me around. The day he was old enough to wield a knife safely would change my life.

"He like Play Dough?"

"Yeah, sure."

"Great." The bowls clanged one by one onto the cool metal counter. "Sugar cookies are just like that. You roll 'em out. You cut shapes. You can't really mess 'em up. And I need a ton for tomorrow."

His faith in me seemed a bit misguided. "Really?"

"Really."

"What are you going to be doing?"

"I'm working on the meat pies. We're going traditional here. Donna wants a bunch of Sicilian meat pies for the luncheon, so that's what we're going to do."

"Meat pies?" Despite having been in the bakery a couple dozen times, I was fairly certain they didn't sell any baked goods with meat in them.

"Yeah. A family recipe. They got pie crust, ricotta, cheese, sauce…"

"Oh! We're making calzones."

He glared at me. "They're *meat pies*. Never mind. Just get

to work. All you need to worry about is the dough. The filling is a family secret."

I held up my rolling pin. "Okay. What you're saying is, if I help with the pies, you'll tell Sheriff Matthews you're not dead?"

"Something like that. Let's get started."

CHAPTER TWENTY-SEVEN

NEVER DID I ever think it would be fun to work in a bakery. After three hours of measuring, sifting, mixing, and pouring, my hypothesis turned out to be spot on. Baking was not the life for me. At least Tony let me "taste test" one of the meat pies so my stomach stopped growling.

It was absolutely amazing.

Not the point.

Somewhere around the fourth hour, Tony seemed to thaw a bit toward me. Nothing appreciable like saying, "Nice job" or "thanks for your help." But he came over to check the thickness of my cookie dough and grunted instead of telling me to start over.

I took that as my opening. "How well do you know Todd LaCroix?"

"Who?"

Not a good sign. "He's your realtor. I saw him earlier today at your house."

"Oh." Tony grunted again. "One of my customers recommended him. Nice enough guy. Talks a good game. Seems like he makes a lot of sales. He listed the house for way too high, I think, but what do I know? He thinks it'll trigger a bidding war."

"Did that upset you?" I asked, trying to sound casual.

"Nah. If the house doesn't sell, maybe Donna's fiancé will let me buy her out. I don't want to move, but that guy is a real piece of work. Asking for way too much money, refusing to let Donna rent her half. She'd do it if he weren't pressuring her."

"Sounds like you're not a fan of the groom." I kept my eyes trained on the rolling pin, not wanting Tony to understand how important this conversation could be.

"I know what you're thinking. No guy is good enough for my baby sister, right? But that ain't it. Alan is a creep. He swoops in, takes over Donna's life, starts changing everything. First he gets her to quit the bakery, then he convinces her to move outta town. Sure, it's not far, but in the winter, the roads are terrible. I'm never gonna—" He stopped abruptly and shook his head. "I'm never gonna get this luncheon done if I keep yammering. Less talk, Tin Foil Girl. Keep mixing. I'll be back soon."

"Where are you going?"

"Does it matter?"

My fraying patience snapped. I was *stuck in a time loop* because of this ingrate. The same day kept taunting me over and over. I'd been killed, watched half the people I loved die, all to save someone I never even liked. Then he tells me none of it matters.

I crossed my arms over my chest and glared back at him. "Considering I'm only here because I found Todd dead in your house and I'm worried you might be next, yeah, it matters. I'm supposed to keep you alive."

If I'd expected some kind of emotional reaction to my shocking revelation, I would have been disappointed. Just a lot of blinking.

Then, finally, "You're joking, right? That's not funny."

"I wish I were." Actually, I wished I'd kept my mouth shut, but that ship had sailed. "I went to your house to see what happened to you, and he had fallen down the basement stairs. Also, your stairs are not structurally sound. You should get them checked."

Tony swore under his breath. "Man, that's terrible. Tad was a putz, but he was decent enough."

"Todd."

"Right. What are you doing out here if you just found a dead guy in my house? You aren't worried I had something to do with it?"

Given my visions and the other events of today, Tony as the killer seemed unlikely. Things I Couldn't Say for $200. "You seem smarter than killing someone and leaving their body in your basement where anyone could find it."

"Thanks, I think." After a moment, he said, "Okay, look. I'm going to the can. Come if you must."

"I'll wait outside."

We left the kitchen and walked across the moonlit path, which wound through the trees. It had snowed recently, making it almost as bright as day where the moon reflected off the ground. It was also even colder than Shady Grove. I shivered, pulling my coat tighter around myself.

Good thing I didn't believe Tony killed Todd, or I'd be worried about being alone with him in a forest in the middle of the night when no one knew where I was.

"Isn't there a bathroom attached to the kitchen?" I asked.

"Ain't there some kind of saying about that? Don't poop where you eat."

"Sorry I asked."

"No one told you to come with me. The kitchen is warmer."

"Nice try, but I'm staying with you." It occurred to me that I might wind up sleeping in the kitchen at this rate. As an uninvited guest, I didn't have a cabin of my own, and it looked increasingly unlikely that I would get home before I needed to sleep.

That was Future Aly's problem. Present Aly couldn't leave Tony to scout nearby hotels. Instead, I followed him up the porch of a small log cabin into the warm, cozy room. These cabins were more luxurious than they looked from the outside.

A queen-sized wooden bed with faux-fur blankets dominated the space. It beckoned like a siren's song. I had been awake for such a long time. Sort of. Tony disappeared through a door on the left wall that must have led to the bathroom. On the right wall was a fireplace with crackling flames beside an overstuffed armchair. Since Tony wouldn't appreciate me stretching out on his bed until he finished his business, I settled into the chair.

Oh, this was nice. Softer than it looked. Warm. Leaning back, I closed my eyes.

A clattering made me bolt upright. The cabin's exterior door flew open. Before I could react, a black-clad arm tossed something through the door. What the—?

A bottle rolled across the wooden planks, headed straight for the fire. Leaping to my feet, I grabbed it. A glass bottle, soaked rag sticking out of one end.

Smelled like gasoline.

Someone had chucked a Molotov cocktail at Tony's fireplace. If he had been the one sitting in the chair, it would have killed him. It would have killed *me*, if I hadn't grabbed it in time.

I raced for the door but skidded to a halt at the doorway. Anyone could have thrown that bottle. They also could be armed. Running after an unknown killer to confront them when no one knew who or where I was struck me as a terrible idea.

Even knowing time should reset again if they killed me, that wasn't a chance I was prepared to take. Dying twice today was enough, thanks. With my luck, the time loop had ended already, and I just didn't know it. For now, I dropped the bottle in the snow beside the porch and pulled out my phone to call 911.

Still no signal. Grr.

Something banged inside the bathroom, and a moment later, the door swung open. Tony stalked across the cabin, face purple with rage. "What do you think you're doing out here? Can't a guy use the toilet in peace?"

With shaking hands, I pointed at where the bottle lay in the snow. He leaned over to look, squatting down to avoid touching the thing. When his nostrils flared, I knew he'd realized what we were looking at.

"Tony? Someone just tried to kill you."

This confirmed that whoever tampered with the basement stairs hadn't been targeting the realtor. Someone definitely wanted to kill Tony. Now, after he showed up at the campsite unharmed, they'd decided to try again.

Who would want to kill the bride's brother at a wedding? Surely there must have been other times and opportunities for murder. Was it about Tony specifically, or did someone want to stop Donna and Alan from getting married?

CHAPTER TWENTY-EIGHT

PUSHING me out of the way, Tony started down the steps, intent on following the person who threw the bottle. Immediately, I went after him. About fifteen feet down the path, it split into two, and he paused.

Each cabin was secluded by design, surrounded by a copse of trees. Following either path would lead to multiple other offshoots and probably half a dozen cabins on either side.

Under normal circumstances, cozy. Right now, irritating. It was impossible to see where our fire-thrower had gone.

Tony shook his fist into the night and yelled. "You're not gonna get away with this!"

"Do you know who might want to hurt you?"

"Sure, I know. Donna's pissed I won't give her my recipes. Her fiancé wants to sell 'em. She thinks he hasn't ruined our lives enough by taking her away from the business and making me sell my house. I keep trying to tell her, she's got another think coming."

Hearing Tony say, "another think" instead of "another thing" raised my opinion of him more than it probably should have. Hashtag nerd problems.

His comment reminded me of something. "Why are you selling if you don't want to?"

"She's not giving me a lot of choice. She's demanding more than the house is worth, which I'm pretty sure is HIS doing. We could split it into two separate deeds, but who wants to share a basement and a driveway with a stranger? There aren't a lot of houses in my price range unless I move to Willow Falls. I don't want to leave the area. Shady Grove is a nice place. I do good business. On a warm day, I walk to work. On a snow day, I go skiing. It's the best of all worlds. Or it used to be, until he came along." Tony strode down the path and I followed. We weren't headed back toward his cabin or the kitchen, so he must be going to find his sister.

My first inclination was to march straight to the lodge and call the police. There had to be a landline at the reservation desk. Someone needed to fingerprint the bottle, run tests, and figure out who was behind this.

Tony absolutely refused. "We're not ruining my little sister's big day by bringing a bunch of police in to run around and mess it all up."

"You don't think it would ruin her wedding when your cabin exploded and you turned up dead?"

"That didn't happen, did it? Listen, we just need to be vigilant. We call the cops, they come in, they track snow and salt all over my kitchen, they stop us from baking, and next thing you know, the meat pies aren't ready for the rehearsal tomorrow. Not happening. Not on my watch."

If we were in Shady Grove, I would ignore this mandate, pick up my phone, and dial 911. But there still wasn't any reception up here, and I'd never gotten the password for the lodge's Wi-Fi so I could make a call that way.

Note to self: if time resets, call the lodge for the password on the drive up.

Breaking into the lodge to get the password was likely to get me in trouble, and if I got dragged away by police officers, there was no one to help Tony. For now, I was stuck being his unwilling-yet-perky bodyguard.

"You're welcome, by the way," I said pointedly. "What if they try again?"

He grinned. "That's what I've got you for, right? My knightress in shining armor?"

Knightress. That wasn't a word, but I liked it. "Right. Sure. But still—"

"I don't wanna hear another word about it, or I'll ban you from the kitchen. Worse, I'll ask Donna to send you home. If you wanna help me, grab your apron."

This was bananas, but I didn't have a lot of options. Rather than freezing my toes while getting nowhere, I followed Tony back to the kitchen.

On the way, my mind went back to the conversation I'd overheard in the stable earlier. Alan needed money. Donna was selling the house she and Tony shared, forcing her brother to move. The sale of the house would give them money, unless they'd heavily mortgaged it. As a private-investigator-in-training, Rusty could look that up for me, but loaning me his car was risky enough. The best way to protect my best friend was to avoid him as much as possible until this was all over.

What else did I know?

Tony didn't want to move. Tony didn't like Donna's fiancé. Donna didn't like Tony meddling in her relationship. Would she kill her own brother?

They'd lived together for years. They'd worked together for ages. By all accounts, they were tighter than me and Rusty. Even knowing Alan wanted to sell Tony's recipes to a grocery store chain, it didn't make sense that Donna would kill to get them.

Unfortunately, I hadn't seen enough at the cabin earlier to tell anything about the person who'd thrown the bottle. Donna was tall with long, curly black hair, but that could easily be concealed with a hat. This time of year, between the hats, the bulky coats, and the boots, everyone looked the same. The person I'd seen could have been her. It could have been Alan. It also could have been Jason Momoa.

Whoever it was, they'd been smart enough to stay on the stone path, meaning I didn't get any footprints to help narrow it down. Maybe we could fingerprint the bottle? Unless it came from the lodge's refrigerator, in which case we'd have to eliminate the prints of Tony and the entire kitchen staff before getting any useful information.

Ugh. Curling my fingers into fists, I kicked the snow. It made me feel about one percent better. I kicked it again.

Given my ability to point at Tony and show him as alive, I felt less worried about calling the police than earlier in the day. But I wanted to be sure I wouldn't get tossed into jail. Now they'd probably add "fleeing arrest" to the list of made-up charges against me. Could a person flee an arrest they were only aware of in an alternate reality?

When we got there, I donned my apron as instructed, picked up a rolling pin, and got back to work. At least rolling out dough gave me a target for my frustration. And I liked stabbing the cookie cutters into place.

Once the warmth from the kitchen seeped back into my bones, I decided to try again to figure this whole mess out.

"Tony, who hates you enough to want you dead?"

"I'm good-looking, I'm smart, I'm Italian. Someone always wants me dead."

"Come on, I'm serious. How can I protect you if I don't know where to look for the danger?" I couldn't tell him about my visions. He'd never believe me. I'd be out in the snow faster than you could say "sodium chloride". My mind went back to the conversation I'd overheard in the stable. "What about Donna's fiancé? You said he wants your family recipes."

"Alan? He's a weasel," Tony said.

"Weasel enough to kill?"

"Nah. He doesn't have it in him. He slinks around, buddying up, trying to trick me into telling him my secrets. Like I'm some kinda sucker. He wants to do a reality show here or some baloney." He snorted.

"Can't he get the recipes from Donna? She must help you bake."

"She doesn't know my secret ingredients. They're pre-mixed, lettered, and labeled. Look." We walked to the large pantry, where row after row of opaque plastic containers lined the shelves. Each one had a large capital letter pasted on the side. No other indication of the contents. My inner scientist appreciated his methodology.

But if I were being asked to make food with them, I'd probably be annoyed not to know what I was using. For a moment, I was on Donna's side.

"Is there a master list your sister could have accessed if Alan pushed her?"

Tony tapped his forehead several times. "Right up here."

My eyes narrowed. "So if you die, Let's Bake a Deal dies with you? No one ever gets to experience those amazing cupcakes again? That's criminal, Tony. Thelma will find a way to bring you back to life only to kill you all over again, and the rest of the town might help."

His face turned red. "Awww, shucks. Okay, fine. There's a record somewhere. Only my lawyer knows where it is. Neither one of us is talking."

"Does Donna inherit the shop when you die?"

"Oh, no. I don't like where you're going with this. My sister loves me, and I love her." Avoiding my eyes, he took the bowl off the stand mixer and grabbed a ladle. One spoonful at a time, he added meat to a row of meticulously rolled, somewhat lumpy pie crusts I'd been working on earlier. "Now close these up."

Rather than argue, I obeyed. The best way to keep him

talking was to comply with these requests. Slowly and steadily, we moved down the row of pies. I waited until we'd finished a dozen of the hand-held pastries, letting him think about our conversation.

Finally, I took a deep breath and asked the one thing I most needed to know. "Does Donna love you more than her future with Alan?"

For the first time since I arrived, Tony stopped and met my eyes. He looked like he'd been punched in the stomach. Since meeting her fiancé, Donna had quit her job with Tony and decided to sell the house they owned together. She was moving away from him.

Realization dawned as he put the pieces together. "No. She couldn't."

But the look in his eyes told me that maybe, just maybe, she could.

CHAPTER TWENTY-NINE

WHEN TONY REALIZED his sister might be the one behind
the attempts on his life, he looked so forlorn, I almost wanted
to hug him. It was like he'd just been told he had to switch to
gluten-free, sugar-free, all-vegan ingredients in every recipe.

"Maybe she didn't have anything to do with it," I
suggested. "She loves you. The two of you worked together
for years. You live under the same roof."

He shook his head. "No. My baby sister believes romantic
love is stronger than anything else. Including family. She'd do
anything for her man. About ten years back, she gave some
boyfriend five thousand dollars to get an inheritance in
Africa. I told her it was a terrible idea, that it wasn't real. She
refused to talk to me for a month, even after it turned out I
was right."

"Tony, we need to call the police."

"Not yet we don't. Donna wants her dream wedding, and
she's going to get it. You're just stirring up trouble." He
grunted. "Enough yammering. We need to get this done."

The fact that he still wanted to finish the desserts raised
my opinion of Tony another notch. But maybe he thought
better when his hands were busy. I did.

As badly as I wanted to call the police, I couldn't shake the feeling that we weren't quite done yet. I'd determined that Tony was alive. I'd saved Todd, but I was missing something. Doug and Sheriff Matthews were certain Tony was dead. Jeff had seen a chalk outline. Was it of someone who looked similar? A glamour? Or did Mary fabricate an entire fake crime scene?

Better to stick by Tony until I figured it out. Heading back to Shady Grove to confront Doug would leave him vulnerable to whoever wanted to hurt him. He obviously wasn't going anywhere with me. Dude was stubborn as a mule and strong as an ox. Plus, there was no reason for the police to believe Tony was alive when I couldn't produce the man in the flesh.

No, the only way to fix this was to finish the job, then appeal to whatever good side Tony had. If he loved his sister, he shouldn't want her to marry the guy who probably tried to kill him. Unless we were making treats to celebrate Alan's pending arrest, this was all very confusing. Was Tony under some kind of spell, too? An "act completely against your own interests" spell?

One by one, we filled the remaining pie crusts and loaded each finished delicacy onto a baker's tray. When the final pan was off the counters, Tony pulled a cover over the whole thing, zipped it shut, and wheeled it toward the giant walk-in refrigerator.

In the morning, he'd come back and bake everything. We both would, I guessed. Assuming time didn't loop on me again. It had to be after midnight. Maybe the curse was finally broken, but I wouldn't believe it until the sun came up. For now, I was too tired to get excited.

After everything was put away and the counters wiped clean, we walked back to the cabin. My mind was still constantly searching for an opening, but it had been a long day. I didn't know what Tony was thinking, but he seemed to have crossed his sister off the suspect list.

Once Tony got to a safe place, I'd pay Donna a visit. That didn't seem like a great plan, but it was all I had. No one else was going to tell me anything until morning, and that might be too late.

Back at Tony's cabin, he ignored me as he walked through the doorway and toward the far wall.

"Where are you going?" I asked.

"It's been a long day. It's late. I'm tired. Someone tried to kill me. You think it might be my only sister." Tony stalked toward the bathroom before turning in the doorway and glaring at me. "I got a tiny, annoying shadow who won't leave me alone and two hundred meat pies to bake tomorrow morning. I'm going to take a shower, get the smell of gasoline offa me, and go to sleep."

"But what—?"

"You think someone's gonna get me in the shower? This ain't the Bates Motel."

I didn't answer. It sounded silly when he said it like that.

"Listen. Take a nap. You've had a long, rough day." He held the door open with one arm. "Unless you want to come in and watch."

Uh, no. Hard pass.

I crossed my arms over my chest. "Thanks. I'll wait out here."

If he thought I was going to lie down and go to sleep while he went gallivanting out into the night, he had another think coming. But after the door slammed and the water turned on, it occurred to me that maybe resting wasn't the worst idea.

After triple-checking the lock on the front door and all the windows, I moved back to my chair by the fire and settled in to watch the flames. Time hadn't reset yet. Maybe I was finally nearing the end of this terrible day. Maybe this time, if I fell asleep, I'd wake up to a rising sun in the woods rather than at 2:57 p.m. in Kevin's front hall.

A sound made me jump in my chair. Some kind of scraping? We were in the woods. It was probably a tree shifting in the wind, moving across the window. But all of a sudden, I felt uneasy.

Standing up, I moved toward the closed bathroom door.

"Tony?" I tried not to sound as anxious as I felt.

No answer.

He'd been in the shower too long. If he really was doing bathroom things, I absolutely didn't want to barge in. But the feeling in my stomach told me that wasn't the case.

With all the force I could muster, I banged on the wooden door. Taking a deep breath, I spoke from my diaphragm. "Tony! Everything okay in there?"

Still nothing.

Pressing my ear to the door, I strained, but all I could hear was the running water. I knocked again. Same result. Finally, taking a deep breath, I squeezed my eyes shut against seeing anything I shouldn't, flung the door open, and waited for Tony's cry of righteous indignation.

Only the sound of running water.

Bracing myself for the sight of a collapsed Tony, I opened my eyes.

The window was open, and Tony was gone.

For a moment, I worried that someone had opened the window, grabbed Tony, and dragged him out of here. But surely, that would have caused quite the racket. Tony wasn't the kind of guy to go meekly with a kidnapper.

He was, however, the kind of guy to ditch me.

Silently, I cursed myself for letting him out of my sight. I should've known he would sneak away. He'd been acting so calm, but all this time, he'd intended to confront Donna. I needed to find them.

After turning off the shower, I checked the ground outside the window. Only one set of footprints marked the snow. Unless someone broke in, took Tony, chucked him over their shoulder, and hauled him away like a sack of potatoes, he'd walked out of here under his own power.

Hmm. Jason Momoa was looking more likely by the second.

Grumbling, I slammed the window shut and turned to head back to the kitchen. I knew he'd been too chill about the possibility of his sister or her fiancé trying to kill him. He must have gone to confront her.

The trail in the snow took me back through the trees. Thanks to the full moon, I managed to navigate the woods without breaking an ankle. The footprints came to a stop at another path. One way snaked further into the woods, and the other headed back in the general direction of the main lodge.

A wooden signpost sat about twenty feet to my right, so I went over to read it. That way, the path would take me to the reception area, the stable, and the parking lot. If I turned right here, I'd head toward the guest cabins, likely including Tony's. Had he just made a circle?

Oh, how I missed the internet. It would take me about eight seconds to find a map of this place.

Tony wasn't trying to hide his tracks. I didn't think he would have gone to the trouble of making a fake trail and doubling back when my attempts to protect him amused him more than anything. Turning around, I followed the path away from the fork, past where Tony's footsteps came out of the woods. After a couple of minutes, I rounded a corner and —a ha!

A very large wooden cabin sat in front of me. Bigger than Tony's. All white, very picturesque. Two hearts and a painted signpost declared this the bridal suite. I bounded up the steps before realizing all the lights were off. It was the middle of the night, after all.

"Tony?" I whispered, hoping he would both hear me and respond. Nothing.

Creeping closer, I listened for any signs of life. No one stirred inside. If Tony came here to confront his sister, he must have changed his mind.

Unless he'd gone to find Alan instead.

The path ended here, so I decided to head back in the direction I came. This wasn't a huge resort. How many cabins could they have?

Too many, it turned out. I found another copse surrounding six units, all cleared of snow but dark. No way to tell if anyone was staying in any of them. No handy fresh footprints. Alan could be anywhere. I couldn't knock on each door, wake the occupants, and ask whoever answered if the bride's brother had dropped by to accuse them of trying to kill him.

With a sigh, I went back to Tony's cabin. It was still empty, which left me two more places to look: the kitchens or the stable. There was no logical reason to think he'd go to the stable. He must have gone to check on the food. Or maybe he was hungry.

When I got to the small stone building housing the kitchen, the windows were unlit. Okay, maybe the stable was the answer after all. Tony couldn't have just disappeared. He had to be here somewhere. I started to go down the hill when something moved out of the corner of my eye. I stopped and waited, hardly daring to breathe.

A bobbing light moved across the row of windows at the top of the kitchen. Someone was in there!

Did Tony think I wouldn't remember he had a flashlight? I was going to grab that man by his greasy hair and drag him out while lecturing him on bad decisions.

As the kitchen door swung open, I stopped. My hand paused halfway to the switches beside the door. Why would Tony not have turned on the light in his own kitchen?

If he came back to check on the pies, he couldn't do that by flashlight. Although I'd love to believe Tony feared me coming in here to lecture him, that didn't make any sense. He probably assumed I'd either fallen asleep waiting for him to come out of the world's longest shower, I was still sitting there waiting for him to come out like a schmuck, or I would help him.

None of those were terrible assumptions.

I expected to find Tony back at the tables where we'd been working earlier, me rolling out dough (poorly) while Tony mixed the filling (expertly). But a glance at that gleaming countertop showed it as empty as when we'd left. What was going on? Where was Tony? Was I about to loop back to 2:57 p.m. because I'd failed again?

A dim light shone from over by the baker's racks where we'd stowed everything until tomorrow. The plastic covering the pastries had been unzipped, with one edge of the plastic moved aside.

Someone wearing jeans and a sweatshirt had pulled out a tray of baked goods. Someone not wearing a white chef's jacket or baker's hat. Someone with straight, dark hair rather than Tony's slicked-back gray locks.

Someone who was tampering with our painstakingly prepared pastries.

CHAPTER THIRTY

MY HEART POUNDED. I'd been looking for someone out to get Tony, but not our pies. There was only one person it could be. Only one person who would want to hurt Tony badly enough to sabotage his baked goods for the wedding luncheon. Which would destroy his relationship with Donna once he hinted that Tony had ruined the meal on purpose.

"Stop!" I tightened my grip on the rolling pin. "Game over, Alan. We know what you're doing."

The man spun around. While he had dark hair like the man I'd seen earlier, his face was oval, with long features and a pointed nose. Even in the dim light, it seemed clear he didn't have a long, jagged scar across one cheek. Or maybe he did—somewhere under the full beard and mustache.

It wasn't the guy I'd spotted through the stable window. Whoever this was, I'd never seen him before in my life. Who was he and what was he doing here?

The intruder laughed at my obvious confusion. "Guess you don't know as much as you think, do you, little girl?"

Nothing made me want to chuck a rolling pin at someone's head more than them calling me "little girl." I resisted only because this guy couldn't tell me anything if he were unconscious. Or if he caught the rolling pin and came after me, which was a much more likely scenario.

Through gritted teeth, I said, "Who are you?"

"Oh, I'm sorry, I should have introduced myself. I'm Greg. It's lovely to meet you. For me, anyway. Not for you." He paused. "I'm sorry to say you're going to get tragically locked in the freezer. A terrible accident. It'll be so sad. With all the trouble that's been happening, people will think this property is cursed. They won't want to come to events anymore, between the food making everyone sick and the chef's assistant dying. I'm so glad you walked in on me! This is perfect."

As he spoke, the man's voice became more and more familiar. Then everything clicked into place. "You're the neighbor. The one who holds the mortgage on this place."

"Ohhh. Smart *and* cute. A double threat. Not to me, obviously. Unfortunately for you, not to anyone in the future."

Greg stood between me and the main exit. To my left were the doors to the walk-in refrigerator and freezer. Behind me was the tunnel leading to the main reception area. I didn't know if I could outrun Greg, but finding out seemed to be my best option. I couldn't hide in the fridge or the freezer without him locking the doors, and with no sign of Tony, I had no idea how long it might be before someone came to let me out.

"Why do you want to hurt Tony?" I asked. "Do you even know him?"

"I don't need to know him," Greg said. "Alan owes me a lot of money. Gave me a mortgage on this place a few years ago. Alan is convinced he can talk Donna into getting enough to pay me back. I was going to kill Tony. If Donna thinks her beloved fiancé killed her brother, she'll break things off. No money for Alan. But every time I tried, Tony got away. Time for Plan B."

That didn't sound right. I tilted my head at him. "Donna

and Tony are selling their house in town. How much does Alan owe you?"

Greg said, "Way more than any house in Shady Grove is worth, I promise you."

"If you just want to get the lodge shut down, you don't need to kill anyone. Why not release a couple of rats in the kitchen and call it a day?" Not that I wanted the Health Department to burst in, but it seemed better than the alternatives.

"I need Alan out of the way. Tony cooks lunch for the entire wedding reception. Everyone gets horribly sick. The assistant is dead. Everyone knows Alan hates Tony. He wants the recipes bad. Bad enough to kill. They'll think he killed you to get them. Once Alan's in jail and the wedding's canceled, there won't be anyone to pay me. Finally, I'll get this place. Rip the whole thing down and put up a luxury resort. It'll be fantastic. I'll make a killing." His beady eyes met mine and he smiled again, a humorless, chilling expression on him. "Pun intended."

Desperately, I decided to bluff. "Tony knows you're trying to take the property from Alan. After I overheard you talking earlier, I told him all about it."

I took a couple of steps away from Greg, toward that swinging door. It was a million miles away and yet also *so close*. All I needed to do was head through the door, down the tunnel, pray the other door wasn't locked from the other side, and then find a landline to call 911.

"Nice try, little girl." Greg took a step toward me. It was now or never. I threw the rolling pin at him, spun without waiting to see if it hit, and ran.

Behind me, Greg roared—whether with anger or pain, I didn't know. Through the swinging door, down the several feet to the main house. Toward the second door. It was unlocked!

Lunging through it, I turned to look for a deadbolt. It was

broken. Greg was still right behind me. I shouldn't have slowed down. Having never been in this room, I didn't know where the nearest exit was. Turning around, I put on a burst of speed—

—and slammed into someone.

A shriek escaped me.

Donna grabbed my arms. "Shh. It's okay. Everything is okay."

"Greg is going to kill us!" I screamed.

"Not today, he's not. Aly, stop. Take a deep breath. Look into my eyes."

Her words finally penetrated my hysterical fog. Flashing blue and red lights played across the room. Turning toward the massive front windows, I saw a police car stopped in front of the lodge. As realization dawned, Doug ran through the front doors and right by me. He barreled through the still-swinging door, headed toward the kitchen.

Inside the hall, Greg turned to go back the other way. Sheriff Matthews appeared in that doorway, sealing Greg's fate. My body sagged with relief.

"How did you know?" I asked.

Her face turned red. "I couldn't sleep, so I went to sneak one of Tony's pies. The oregano, the ricotta… Those pies are so good; they always help relax me. Tony refused to give me one earlier, but I figured he wouldn't notice just one missing."

"Trust me, he would." I laughed at the mental image of him counting every single pastry. "But he would have forgiven you. Especially now that you've saved his legacy. I'm just sorry your pies are ruined."

"Don't be." She held up a paper towel that smelled suspiciously like garlic, tomato sauce, and butter. "I was wrapping this up when I saw the flashlight outside the front door. I thought it was my brother, so I hid. By the time I realized what Greg was doing, you'd caught him. At least I got one. And I'm glad I was here to save you."

"Me, too."

"Me, too." Behind me, Tony spoke. I jumped, not having realized he was there. "I'd hate to lose my assistant. Especially now. We've got two hundred new pies to make."

"You were there the whole time?" I put my hands on my hips. "What was the plan? Let Greg kill me instead of you?"

His face turned red. "I was in the walk-in. Where, incidentally, I would have died with you if you hadn't gotten away."

"Gee, thanks for coming to my rescue!"

"You were doing fine on your own. I would have jumped in if you needed me. Someone needed to catch his confession to give to the cops." He nudged me with one elbow and lowered his voice. "If anyone asks, you authorized me to record that conversation on my phone, okay?"

My lawyer brother would probably have pointed out that he should have asked for permission before making a recording. I simply nodded.

"Hey, Aly?"

Turning around, I found Doug standing behind me. My first instinct was to give him the finger, but he wasn't the bad guy here. "Yeah?"

"Look, we owe you an apology—"

"No. Your uncle maybe, but not you."

"I should have tried harder to convince him you didn't do anything," he said.

"Listen, this one wasn't your fault," I said. "Someone staged the whole thing. You did what you were trained to do."

"There's one thing I don't understand," Doug said.

"What's that?"

"Uncle Tim saw Tony's body. He called the coroner. He took pictures. If it wasn't Tony, who was it?"

That was an excellent question. "Does Tony have a brother?"

"No," Donna said. "Just me."

"One sister is enough," Tony said.

"Not a relative." Doug spoke very slowly. "About an hour ago, the coroner's office called. The body disappeared. His table was empty, tools were clean and put away. Like no one had ever been there. You wouldn't have any idea how that happened, would you?"

Honesty was usually the best policy, but explaining to Doug that someone put a spell on Shady Grove to trap me in a time loop? Yeah, no.

"I've heard that sometimes a gas leak can cause hallucinations," I said. "Someone should go check Tony's bakery, just in case."

Beside me, he started to protest, but I elbowed him.

"This wasn't a hallucination. This was something else." Doug sighed and shook his head. "Another inexplicable happening in Shady Grove. Don't go anywhere, okay? We need to get your statement after I get this guy into the car."

After we agreed, albeit begrudgingly on my part, Doug headed through the far end of the tunnel, presumably to where his uncle had taken Greg.

Donna said, "I've got to go tell Alan what happened. Thank you so much, Aly. You saved our wedding. We'd love to have you as part of our big day. Will you stay to celebrate?"

"Thanks, but I've got to get home. I'm beat."

If my hypothesis was correct, my task today had been to either keep Todd alive or save Tony and prove my innocence. After everything that happened here, the time loop spell should now be satisfied—which meant Sam would be arriving at my house in a few hours. The place probably looked like the police had tossed it searching for evidence.

Besides, I still had a spell to perform. If this day taught me nothing else, Mary needed to be contained immediately. She was too dangerous.

For the first time, I worried the spell wouldn't contain her, even if she were in jail. What would we do then? If there was some kind of magical police force, I didn't know how to contact them. Mrs. Patel's binding spell would have to be enough.

Tony paused in the doorway to look back at me before following his sister. "You're not a terrible assistant, after all."

Considering the source, that was high praise. "Aw, that's sweet, Tony. And I'm glad you're not dead."

"I guess I owe you one. Listen, next time you come in to buy cupcakes, I'll consider negotiating with you." He stabbed one finger in my direction. "Just don't insult me with your opening offer."

I snorted, but he was gone before I could reply. Gloating at the handcuffed guy being loaded into the back of a police car wasn't a great look, but since Greg had tried to kill Tony at least twice, killed Todd by mistake, and lobbed a Molotov cocktail at me, who could blame him? My sympathy was limited.

According to the clock on the wall, it was almost two o'clock in the morning. What now? Should I wait here? Look for a place to sleep? Should I head back to Shady Grove and see what was waiting for me?

No, Doug said to stick around until I could give a statement. Maybe I should call Kevin. If the time loop had ended, I might be able to reach him. But it also seemed silly to wake him in the middle of the night—and Kyle—just to tell him that, hey, everything is fine!

Maybe I should insist they talk to me before any of the other witnesses. After all, I got the confession. I almost died. That should get me some special treatment, right?

I desperately wanted to go home.

My stomach growled. Other than one small meat pie, I hadn't eaten in a very long time. While I waited, I might as well find some food. The pies may be ruined, but the caterers had been cooking all day. Not to mention the cookies I'd been rolling and cutting.

Inside the fridge, I found a bin of leftover meatballs from the cocktail hour earlier. Just looking at them made my mouth water. I didn't care that they were cold. At that point, I barely cared if they were poisoned. I'd lived this day a dozen times, what was one more?

After cramming about twenty of them in my mouth, I felt much better. Time to find Doug and see if they were ready to talk to me. I put the remaining meatballs back where I found them and headed for the outside door. A few feet from the refrigerator, my foot hit something, and I stumbled.

The rolling pin I'd chucked at Greg earlier skittered across the floor. So that's where it landed. Rather than leave it for someone else to trip over, I'd better put it in the sink. I refused to do dishes in the middle of the night, though. You had to draw the line somewhere.

I picked up the rolling pin and headed for the large double basin. Suddenly, the door flew open. It bounced off the wall with a loud crash. Spinning around, I jumped and raised the pin. A second later, Kevin raced into the room.

What was my brother doing here? I was so surprised, I couldn't speak.

His eyes moved wildly around the room until he spotted me. Then he raced toward me and wrapped me in a massive hug. "Oh, thank goodness you're okay!"

"Kevin? What are you doing here? Is Kyle okay?"

He pulled me closer for a moment before letting go. "Kyle is fine. He's with Mrs. Patel."

"In Boston, presumably?"

"No, we came home. We had to. I texted you when we got to the hotel, as promised. You didn't respond. That didn't feel right. I called, and it wouldn't go through. I tried calling Amira or Olive or Sam, and all three numbers gave me the same 'Your call cannot be completed' message. Emma answered her phone, but she said she couldn't get in touch with you. When Rajini couldn't reach her daughter, either, we turned around and came straight back."

My brother's care both touched and infuriated me. "Kevin! This whole weekend is about protecting Kyle. How could you—?"

"Shh. He's fine. He's with Mrs. Patel. They're both fine," he said. "But I needed to make sure you were okay."

"How did you even find me?"

"I didn't. Kyle found Rusty's car. Rusty didn't know where it was after you took it."

Of course. A handy skill, my nephew's power to find lost things.

I opened my mouth to say so, but the room flickered around us. Hopefully not the electricity; I'd had enough of that at Amira's shop earlier. No, wait. This was different.

All the light rushed out, then came back in a brilliant white flare. For a second, I couldn't breathe. Then everything flashed back to normal.

What was happening? My heart thundered. In a way, it felt like the times I reset to the beginning of the time loop, but I was definitely still here in the kitchen. To convince myself, I patted the counters, then my apron, my hair, my arms.

Did I have a seizure?

An amused voice cut into my thoughts. "Well, well, well. I see the police have made an arrest, and our crotchety baker is alive. Looks like you figured it out. Good job. I knew you could do it."

I whirled around, brandishing Tony's rolling pin like a sword. There she was, just as I'd suspected. One of the Towne cousins.

Mary and Priscilla were nearly identical, a fact that never escaped me.

Three women with very similar features. One dead, two alive. One with slightly more hazel eyes, the other a slightly squarer face. After examining lots of pictures and meeting them each in person, I was fairly certain I was staring into the face of a murderer.

My brother stepped forward. He spoke with one hundred percent certainty. "Hello, Mary."

"Hello, Kevin. Hi, Aly. It's nice to see you again."

CHAPTER THIRTY-ONE

MY GRIP TIGHTENED on the rolling pin. I lifted it over my head like a baseball player waiting for the pitch. "Tell me something. If I kill you, will I automatically reset to the start of today? Because it might be worth having to dodge police all over again."

Kevin put a hand on my arm. When he spoke, his voice was low. "Aly…"

Mary laughed. "I guess I deserve that. To be honest, I'm not sure what would happen. Maybe. You might be caught in the time loop forever without me to end it. Living this day over and over, rolling meat pies endlessly like Sisyphus."

It took a minute for her words to sink in. I never expected she would admit what she'd done to me so easily.

"I can't believe you're so cavalier about abusing your powers. I thought one of the basic tenets of witchcraft is Do No Harm. Does that somehow not apply to the famous Towne family?"

"I'm trying to *undo* harm. You keep getting in my way." She gritted her teeth and stepped toward me, hands balled at her sides. "Why couldn't you let me have Kyle so I can fix everything?"

I blinked at her, surprised. What was she playing at now? She wanted to make things right, and that required Kyle. But how?

As if reading my thoughts, Kevin said, "What are you talking about? You know I'd never let you hurt Kyle."

She sighed in exasperation. "I don't want to *hurt* him. Don't you get it?"

For the first time, I really looked at her. It had been several months since I last saw Mary, and the primary thing that had struck me every time was her resemblance to her sister. Same chestnut curls and heart-shaped lips inherited by Kyle. Similar bone structure.

Now I also noticed the deep shadows under Mary's eyes, how limply her hair hung around her face where it escaped its ponytail. She'd lost weight since I last saw her. To be blunt, she looked at least as bad as I must, and I'd gotten arrested for murder, watched half my friends die, and been forced to bake for hours while reliving the same day over and over.

"Of course we don't get it!" I empathized with her misery, but I'd reached my limits. "How is creating a time loop that gets me killed and/or sent to jail supposed to undo harm? The only harm that got undone was the harm you caused! If you hadn't framed me for killing Tony in the first place, there wouldn't have been any need for the loop."

"Look, I'm sorry about that. I really am. I never wanted to hurt you."

I barked out a laugh. She blinked at me. "Sorry. I assumed that was a joke because it's the most ridiculous thing I've ever heard."

"You don't understand. I admit, I hurt you. But everything I did—all of it—was for my sister. All I ever wanted was to save Katrina."

My grip on the rolling pin tightened. My eyes darted around the room, seeking any trap, any advantage. "Let me see if I've got this straight. Over the past year, you've planted a cursed object in my home, cast a spell to steal my powers, and trapped me in this nightmare." I gestured around me. "All to save your sister, who has been dead for more than two years?"

She opened her mouth to speak, but I cut her off.

"Excuse me, I meant to say: who you murdered two years ago."

Mary jerked as if I'd slapped her. "I didn't mean to kill her. It was an accident. I want to make things right."

Beside me, Kevin gasped. "Say that again."

"You can't," I said. "It's not possible."

"I promise you, I can. I have a plan."

I stole a glance at Kevin, whose face had turned white. My brother had the ability to see lies. If Mary wasn't trying to fix things, if she came to hurt me, he would know.

Almost imperceptibly, he nodded. She was telling the truth. I still had about a billion questions, but I tilted my head just enough to tell Kevin I'd gotten the message. Mary wasn't aware of Kevin's powers, and we preferred to keep it that way. She might be here to convince us she wasn't the enemy, but she wasn't close to a friend.

Still wary, I lowered the rolling pin a fraction of an inch. Mostly because my arms were aching. My self-defense lessons hadn't involved holding heavy objects over my head for extended periods of time.

"I don't understand. When I visited her at Destiny's Haven, Priscilla told me you wanted Kyle to do a spell. What spell could be more important than your own sister's life?"

Mary wrinkled her forehead. "Huh?"

"When I scried the past, you wanted to take Kyle. Katrina wouldn't let you. Priscilla said—"

"We should sit down." Instead of moving toward a stool, Mary opened the fridge, pulled out a bottle of wine, and set three glasses on the counter. Then she pointed the bottle at me. "Care to join me?"

In a thousand lifetimes of poor judgment, I would not accept anything that woman gave me to eat or drink. Even knowing I could flounder my way back here wouldn't make it worth finding myself back in the front entryway for the eighty-seventh time. "No, thanks. I don't drink."

"A wise choice." She poured herself a glass and took a swig before settling into a seat. "Alcohol can have strange effects on your powers. I've developed a tolerance, as long as I don't have too much, but poor Prissy gets horrible problems."

"Is that why you locked her up in Destiny's Haven?" Kevin asked.

She sighed and rubbed her temples. "I didn't want to do that, but I didn't have a choice. After Kat died, Prissy snapped. Drank too much, lost her grip on reality. She had to be locked up for her own protection and Kyle's."

That didn't make any sense to me. "What do you mean?"

"My cousin gets visions, like you. But her visions are of the future. Not only the existing future, but lots of possible futures. That's where I got the vision of you killing Tony, by the way."

There was an alternate reality where I really did kill Tony with a rolling pin?

No. Not now.

"We'll come back to that," I said. "Go on."

"I'm sure Priscilla believed whatever she said to you, but she no longer had a clear picture of anything by the time you met her. She'd been slowly deteriorating because she blamed herself."

"But it was you I saw in the mirror," I insisted. "I saw your tattoo."

"I'm getting to that," Mary said. "On the day Katrina died, I went to her house because Priscilla got a vision of her death. I was beside myself. I was prepared to do anything to keep her alive. Priscilla told me there was one way to avoid her vision, a spell to fix everything. I needed a strong power source linked to the family. To do that, I needed Kyle. Need Kyle, in fact, because I still haven't completed that spell."

Mary closed her eyes for so long, I considered grabbing Kevin and slipping away. But my need to give him—and his son—closure kept me rooted to the spot. I hardly dared to breathe, afraid she would change her mind about talking.

Finally, she sat up straight, opened her eyes, and drained the rest of her wineglass. "It was only after I got there, after Katrina attacked me, that I realized the truth. Katrina thought I'd come to hurt her son. In sending me to their house to stop her from dying, Priscilla inadvertently made it happen. She didn't mean to, but she did."

Kevin let out a choking sound and fell back against the counter.

That revelation stunned me into silence. Oh, man. Imagine that someone told you the person you loved most in the world was going to die, and you believed them. You thought you could save them, and then you killed them instead.

What a tragedy.

Part of me wanted to give her a big hug, stroke her hair, and tell her everything would be okay. But my inner scientist remained skeptical. Sure, Kevin said she wasn't lying. But this was so out there, so beyond my comfort zone, I needed to hear something reassuring from Mary's lips.

"Why should I believe you?" I asked.

"For one thing, if I really wanted to hurt you, I would." She snapped her fingers.

The rolling pin in my hand turned to floppy rubber. It melted away from me, oozing through my fingers and dripping onto the floor. Ew.

I went to wipe my hand on my pants.

She snapped her fingers again and suddenly, I sat on top of the kitchen counter, ten feet from where I'd started. Kevin sat beside me, looking as shocked as I felt. At least the goo on my hands was gone.

"How did you do that?" he asked.

"I've spent the past two years growing my magic. I tried to do the spell last year, but I wasn't strong enough yet. Now, I should be able to manage."

"Does that mean you're not going to steal my powers again?" I fired at her.

"Sorry about that. I needed the boost. The rocking horse should have been enough. If you'd given it to Kyle, I would have received a temporary transfer of his abilities. But you gave it to someone else, apparently. The powers I got weren't of our blood. I couldn't use them."

Olive. I'd asked my boss to test the rocking horse with her magic before giving it to Kyle. It attacked her. She'd recovered, thankfully. Just like Jeff recovered after Mary trapped him in rabbit form.

If she wanted to hurt me and my family, she was almost comically inept. Score one point in the "her heart was in the right place" column.

"And the time loop? Why did you make me relive this whole day over and over? I get if you wanted to save Todd's life, but maybe you could have given me a heads up?"

"Who?" Kevin asked.

"Todd LaCroix," I said. "Tony's realtor."

Mary's cheeks turned pink. "When you put it like that, it seems so obvious."

"Yeah. Communication. Talking. Cooperation. All things you might want to look up."

"Listen, I'm sorry," she said. "I've been looking for a house in Shady Grove. I wanted to be nearby if things worked out. Todd's my realtor. Tony's place would be perfect, because it's got a unit for me and one for Prissy. We could be together but separate."

"So Priscilla killed the realtor?" Kevin asked. "I'm so confused."

"No. We were at a showing when she had a vision. She said the house was booby-trapped, and I was going to die on the basement stairs. She got nervous. Todd went down there to show us it was perfectly safe." She blinked and looked away. "I felt terrible. I wanted to fix it."

"Again, I ask: why not just talk to me?"

She shrugged. "I was hyper-focused on finding Kyle so I could do this spell. I wanted to save Todd, but I *needed* to be sure you didn't get in my way. I'd been thinking about how to distract you all morning. If I'd called and told you to go to Tony's house, you wouldn't. But if Tony was dead and people thought you killed him, that would probably get you through the front door to find Todd."

My mind boggled at her thought process. To think whipping up a spell to disrupt my whole day, co-opt the entire Shady Grove Sheriff's Department, and kill my friends one by one in front of me—albeit temporarily—was easier than having a conversation. Instead of commenting, I glanced at Kevin.

"As ridiculous as all this sounds," he said. "I believe her."

Amazing.

"Do me a favor, Mary," I said. "Next time you need help with something: ask. Do not do a spell until we talk."

"I'll agree for now, but only because I still need your cooperation."

Kevin let out a low sound that sounded dangerously close to a growl. "You will never do anything like this again. If you touch Kyle, I will break your arms."

"I will help you," I said. "But you need to leave us alone after this. And I'm still furious with you."

"I completely understand. I'm furious with myself. But you should know nothing I've done to you compares to the misery I've put myself through."

It was hard to feel sorry for her, but I felt a twinge deep inside. Mary had done a lot of terrible things, but she was suffering, too. She wasn't evil, just incredibly misguided.

"Why not talk to me?" Kevin asked. "We were family. Right after Katrina died, I would have trusted you."

"For one thing, I figured you would think I was crazy. You didn't have a psychic sister and son back then. Katrina told me you didn't know about our family. And I guess part of me wanted to make things right on my own. Like, if I could fix this, I might deserve to be forgiven."

"And you could finally forgive yourself," I said.

"There's one thing that still doesn't make any sense to me," I said. "What about your accusations attacking my brother?"

Her face turned red as she averted her eyes. "I couldn't have people wondering if I'd done it, could I?"

"You could have kept your mouth shut and commiserated together," I pointed out.

"Okay, fine, I made a mistake there. I wasn't thinking clearly, remember? But I had a plan."

"A plan that involved me going to jail?" Kevin asked. His tone was almost conversational, but from the set of his jaw, the way he held himself so still, I knew he was furious.

"Yeah. Or what if he got fired?" I asked. "Did your plan consider any of those things?"

"Again, it shouldn't matter. We do the spell, Katrina comes back. Kevin can't get in trouble, because she's not dead."

We were changing the world. That gave me pause. In the past two years, I'd moved to a new town, made new friends, strengthened my relationship with my brother several times over, developed a close bond with my nephew, fallen in love, met an amazing mentor, discovered my psychic powers and how to use them—would any of it matter? What if I lost it all?

On the other hand, because of my bonds with Kevin and

Kyle, I would give anything to bring Katrina back. Even if that meant never meeting Olive or Sam.

Never meeting Sam? Tears sprang to my eyes.

In whatever future arose, I could move back to Shady Grove, meet Olive again. Kevin would still be nearby. Olive would still own the antique store. We could talk. We wouldn't have the same relationship maybe but—how could I trade my sister-in-law's life for a bond with a stranger that could be reforged?

The thought of losing Sam hurt more. He was the yin to my yang. He picked me up when I was down, brightened every day, and helped me without question any time I asked. I loved him, and I liked who I was when we were together. The thought of giving him up…

But Sam was *alive*. Katrina was dead. No one was asking me to trade his life for hers. How could I go on raising Kyle knowing that I could have brought his mother back to life, but I didn't because I wanted to spend more time with my boyfriend? We'd only started dating a few months ago.

If we were meant to be, we'd find each other again. I had to believe that.

We'd also be taking away Kevin's current relationship. Oh, man. That couldn't be my call.

"Kev? What about Julie?"

He thought for a long moment. "I care about her. I don't want to hurt her. But Katrina was my person. If we could bring her back, how can I possibly say no?"

"You won't hurt Julie," Mary cut in. "She'll never know you started dating unless you met and fell for her in that world."

He shook his head firmly. "I wouldn't. I'd never stop looking for Katrina. But, Aly, what about your life?"

"I'll still have a life," I said, sounding more sure than I felt. "I was already looking at transferring to Maloney College. If

Katrina's missing, all the more reason to enroll. Mary, will I remember all of this?"

"You will. I will. Only the people doing the spell, though," she said. "No one else."

I could live with that. I had to live with it. We could go around and around in circles all day, but I'd never be able to look myself in the mirror if I had a chance to make my sister-in-law not dead and I walked away from it.

Kevin turned to me. "Aly, are you sure? I can't ask you to give up everything for me."

"You're not asking," I said. "I'm offering."

"I know how you feel about Sam."

"And I know how you felt about Katrina. Kyle deserves to know his mother."

My brother's eyes filled with tears. "I can never repay you."

"I'll put it on your tab," I said. "Mary, I will help you, on two conditions."

"Anything."

"First, we don't tell Kyle. Not now, not ever. Win or lose. I can't do that to him."

"That's impossible. We need Kyle to work the spell."

"Actually, I don't think you do." The skeptical side of my brain screamed at me not to tell Mary what I was about to say. But I'd already decided to trust her. She had more power than I could dream of, and if she wanted to hurt me, she could. The orb protected Kyle, not me. Before I could change my mind, I said, "I've got something to tell you."

She narrowed her eyes at me. "Don't think for a second you can trick me into believing you've got that kind of power."

I shook my head. "Oh, no. Not me. I have something better. Before she died, Katrina created an orb and put her essence into it. It was supposed to protect Kyle. And as far as I know, it has."

Mary swore under her breath. "I knew it! Prissy said I was imagining things, but I knew it! That's why my last spell backfired."

"Backfired? You caused an earthquake and drained magic from half the town," Kevin said.

"Sure, but I didn't get *Kyle's* strength. That was the point of the spell."

"What would have happened to him? Would he have gotten his powers back?" I asked.

She hesitated and bit her lip. Finally, when I was just about ready to call the whole thing off, she shook her head. "I don't know. But I was willing to risk it. He's a kid. He'd never miss them. Not like he misses his mother. Are you still going to help me?"

It was too late to back out now that she knew about the orb. If I said no, she'd probably reset the time loop and find another way to get it. At least if we worked together, I could keep my eye on her. "Yeah. Just one more thing."

"What's condition number two?"

"If the spell fails—that's it. You leave us alone. Leave Shady Grove, leave New York. I don't want you near us ever again."

Mary swallowed. "Never?"

I crossed my arms over my chest. "I understand how terrible you feel. I loved Katrina, too. I want to bring her back. But I also love Kyle. He deserves to grow up like a normal little boy, as much as possible. If this doesn't work, you need to stay away from him."

She gazed at me with narrowed eyes. At first, I thought she would refuse. After all, she didn't need me. I didn't have Kyle's abilities. But I was her path to the orb. If she didn't grant me this one request, she'd never get it—or Kyle.

Finally, her face relaxed. She nodded tightly. "The spell won't fail. I agree."

"Great! When should we do it?"

"Right now."

"Are you kidding? It's after midnight. I've lived about four thousand times today. I'm exhausted."

"You can sleep in the car. Besides, I don't need you if I have the orb." She paused. "Today is the anniversary of Katrina's death. The two dates that will give us the best chance of success are today and her birthday. I could do the spell on her birthday but, well, that's not until February. More than anything, I want to spend Christmas with my sister."

I'd cut off my arm and hand it to her before letting her take that orb away from me, but that statement made me feel a lot better about helping her. Christmas was in a few weeks. If we brought Katrina back, we'd have more to celebrate. My parents were planning to spend the holidays with us, and it would be that much better if Katrina could be with us.

"I'm coming with you. What else do you need to get ready?"

"We need to go to Kevin and Katrina's old house."

Of all the things she might have said, I never expected to hear that. "In Star's Ridge? That's three hours away."

"Then I guess you'll get plenty of time to nap in the car."

"As if I'd trust you to drive me anywhere," I grumbled.

"You don't have a choice."

She had me there, but I didn't have to like it.

"Why can't we do it at my house?" I asked.

"Because Katrina's energy is strongest in the house where she died."

"What if the owners catch us breaking into their house to do magic?"

"I can put them in a time freeze like this one. If the spell works, it won't matter," Mary said. "We'll revert to the 2022 we all would have lived if Katrina had never died, and the house will presumably still belong to her and Kevin."

"And if it doesn't work?"

Her eyes filled with tears. "Then nothing matters."

CHAPTER THIRTY-TWO

SINCE I HADN'T BROUGHT anything to the resort with me, it only took a minute to get ready to leave. I grabbed a handful of cookies from the fridge, and Kevin warned Mary that he would make her pay if she double-crossed me. Then he left to be with Kyle. I waited until he was out of sight before taking Mary to Rusty's car.

Despite my better judgment, I climbed into the passenger seat. It wasn't safe for me to get behind the wheel when this tired, and we couldn't stick around while I slept.

Once we turned out of the parking lot and onto the road, Mary lifted the time freeze she'd put on everyone else at the resort.

"Won't the police wonder where I disappeared to?" I asked. "I was, after all, their key witness."

"Oh, don't worry. You're still there, waiting to give a statement."

"What?"

"Everyone here sees a copy of you. A memory, really. It will answer their questions and then fade away."

I probably should've been outraged that she'd copied me, but I didn't have the energy. My first reaction was a massive wave of relief. After the day I'd had, I didn't want to talk to anyone. Especially not the police, even if Doug was a friend. If I turned around now, we'd be stuck there for hours. All I wanted was to go home.

Which reminded me, I needed to make a call.

When I pushed the phone button on my dashboard, Mary grabbed my wrist. "Hold on. What are you doing?"

"Sam's going to be at my house in a few hours, expecting to see me. I can't let him show up and find everything the way the police left it."

She thought for a moment before letting me go. "When is he due?"

"Why? Are you going to send a copy of me to meet him?" For a second, she looked like she was considering it. "I was joking! Don't you dare."

"No, I was going to say, it shouldn't matter. If he's arriving after lunch, we will have already done the spell."

We will have done the spell…and switched over into a reality where my boyfriend might not know me.

No. I couldn't go there. Talk of Sam reminded me of something else I wanted to ask her. "Hey, I've got a question. Earlier, you blocked me from calling Kevin, right? And Mrs. Patel, Emma, everyone?"

"Yeah. You could only reach people in Shady Grove."

"Then how could I call Sam?"

"You couldn't."

"But I did," I said firmly.

She stopped the car and looked at me. "What are you talking about?"

"My boyfriend lives in New York City. Earlier today, I called him. After the time loop started. After I'd looped a bunch."

Her brow furrowed. "That shouldn't be possible."

"Then what happened?"

She was quiet for so long, I almost fell asleep.

"I can think of two possibilities," she said finally. "The first is that your boyfriend has his own magic. Something that lets him protect you."

Although I'd considered many times that Sam might have some inherent abilities like his mother's and mine, the idea of him being magic and not telling me didn't feel right. "What's the other?"

She smiled. "He must truly and deeply love you. If your connection is more powerful than my spell, he could reach you through it."

"Oh, wow. Yeah. He's really something." Her words filled me with warmth. Then I remembered that, if this spell worked as planned, I might be throwing that connection away.

That thought punched me in the gut.

No. I had to believe we'd find each other again.

To keep from dwelling on the possibilities, I asked, "How does this work, anyway? Is this like in *The Avengers*, where they go back in time and create new realities? So we're living in a time where Katrina never died, but there's another Aly and Kevin and Kyle who are without her now?"

"No. Going back in time to change things would create a paradox, and nature doesn't like paradoxes. If we try that and fail, I won't have the strength to try it again. Then we'll miss our window and have to wait another year." Her voice cracked. "I can't wait another year to see my sister. I just can't."

"I understand. What's the plan?"

"We're going to fold the fabric of reality. I'm going to bend time and reach into the past to find Katrina before she died and bring her into the present. To everyone living in 2020, including you and me, it will seem as if she went missing. Then, violá! In 2022, she's been found."

"And no one will remember the last two years." She'd mentioned this earlier, but I hadn't fully processed it. Would I be living in Shady Grove? I had been thinking about transferring to Maloney College before Katrina died, but nothing had been set in stone. What if we did this and I found myself magically transported back to Sacramento?

"You and I will." She paused. "Whether the spell works or not, we should be finished before Sam gets to your house. There's no need to call him yet."

Briefly I considered asking him to meet us at Kevin and Katrina's old place, if for no other reason than to make sure Mary couldn't pull a fast one. But she had every opportunity to kill me, first at the resort and now that we were alone in the car. Which reminded me.

"How did you get to the resort in the first place? You don't have a broomstick, do you?"

She laughed. "Don't be ridiculous. I took an Uber. Quite the bill, let me tell you. But by tomorrow, it should be erased."

According to that philosophy, maybe we should stop and buy a Porsche or two before heading south. We could travel in style *and* avoid a massive monthly payment.

"We need to make one stop on the way," she said.

No matter how I pressed, she refused to say any more about our detour. Eventually I leaned against the window and closed my eyes. It was easier not to argue, and I was exhausted.

By the time Mary stopped the car in front of a very fancy hotel in Saratoga, I felt much better. Like I'd slept at least forty-five minutes.

"Wait here," she said. "I'll be right back."

"If police surround the car, and I reset to my entryway at 2:57, I am going to be very cross with you," I told her.

She smirked but didn't respond. I watched her in the side view mirrors as she disappeared into the lobby. A moment later, she returned. Except now there were two of her. Did she make a copy of herself, too?

No. Of course not. This woman's heart-shaped lips, brown eyes, and slightly oval face told me exactly who she was.

"Priscilla," I said when she opened the rear car door. "I should have known."

"How have you been, Aly?" she asked.

"To be honest, I'm rather displeased with you at the moment. I trusted you! We were supposed to help each other, and then you ditched me."

"We are," she said. "I'm here to help Mary with the spell. She needs as much Towne energy as possible. Besides, the two of us have always been stronger together."

"Why didn't you tell me that when we met at Destiny's Haven?"

"I didn't know if I could trust you."

These women were so frustrating. If this worked, it would be worth it. But—

"I thought she lost her mind," I said to Mary when she climbed back behind the wheel. "Isn't that what you told me?"

"Feel free to talk about me like I'm not here," Priscilla muttered. "I don't mind."

Mary shushed her. "My cousin had a hard time after Kat died. But we've been working together, and she's doing much better. We need her to work the spell. Even with the orb."

The sun was beginning to peek over the horizon, filling the air with pink streaks. Although it had been past midnight for several hours, seeing the sun rise finally made me feel like I'd survived. Time wasn't going to reset on me again. That reassured me more than anything Mary said.

On the way to Star's Ridge, Mary and Priscilla told me stories about growing up with Katrina.

"Did she have magic?" I asked. "For some reason, I thought no. But then she made the orb and left it with Mallory."

"She went through a period where she tried to deny it," Mary said.

"We all did," Priscilla added. "Katrina's lasted a long time. I think she met your brother and wanted to try living a 'normal life.'"

That seemed odd because my brother also had psychic powers, but maybe he'd never gotten a chance to tell her. It could have been a part of himself he wanted to hide. Especially if he didn't know she had magic, too. But it also explained why they were drawn to each other.

I didn't mention that. Kevin's story wasn't mine to tell. While Mary and Priscilla knew I was psychic, I'd never told them about him.

"Then why did she make the orb?" I asked.

"I called her," Priscilla said. "When I had the vision, I called to warn her that her life was in danger."

"You didn't cause her death, Prissy. I've told you a million times," Mary said.

"I know, I know. But maybe she wouldn't have attacked you if she didn't think she was about to die." She sounded wistful. "I guess we'll never know."

"That's not true," Mary said. "In about half an hour, you can ask her."

In this neighborhood, people apparently got ready for Christmas early. Some of the houses already had put up lights. While they might have left them up year-round, the house at the end of the block also boasted a family of snowmen and a dancing Rudolph. Festive, yet weird. Christmas wasn't for three weeks.

While I was gaping, Mary turned into the massive circular driveway of a modern-day McMansion. It looked the same as I remembered it, right down to the statue in the middle of the front yard and the white columns on either side of the front double door. It was beautiful, but I preferred our Shady Grove house. This was much too formal for my tastes. No

Christmas lights here, so the new owners must be waiting for a reasonable time to put them up.

A piece of cardboard covered a hole the living room window. The new owners must have kids. Thankfully, all the lights were off. I didn't completely understand how Mary's time spell worked.

"Did anyone steal a key?" Priscilla asked.

"I was going to break a window," Mary said. "Although it appears someone already did that for us. We can climb through."

"No need," I said, pointing at the front door. "They've got a coded entry. I can open it."

"Very handy," Mary said.

If I didn't know better, I'd have thought she was impressed. "You swear the owners won't jump out and call the police?"

"Cross my heart," she said. "Time is frozen for everyone but us."

The two of them unloaded the trunk while I went up to work on the front door. Kevin's old code didn't work, not surprisingly. But it only took a minute to call up a vision and get the new one.

Mary directed us to set up in the foyer, in the spot where Katrina died. We placed candles around the room and lit incense. Priscilla spread petals in a large circle around the three of us, then added a second layer of sand. At Mary's direction, I set a mirror in the center of everything, then placed the orb on top of it.

"Does it always glow that brightly?" Priscilla asked.

"Usually it's more of a shimmer," I said. "I think this place gives it power."

"That's a good sign." Mary took a deep breath. "Everyone ready?"

The three of us sat on the floor, being careful not to disturb the circle of salt. One by one, we lit the candles. Mary unfolded a large piece of fabric and handed one corner to me, one to Priscilla. With a start, I recognized it as part of Katrina's wedding dress. Mary must have gone into Kevin's storage unit to get it. The fourth corner of the white silk fluttered in the air above the orb.

Mary looked up to the ceiling, took a deep breath, and began to speak rapidly in Latin. I didn't understand all the words, but I recognized a few from my studies with Olive.

"As we fold this fabric, so to fold the fabric of reality," Mary said in English. "Take us back to the person who made this orb. Use her essence."

Priscilla handed her corner of the dress over to Mary, who folded them together. She reached for mine. I put it in her hand, feeling a tug of magic. Something was definitely happening.

"Show me Katrina!" Mary called to the sky.

Priscilla clapped her hands loudly.

Thunder cracked around us. A flash of light streaked out of the orb, opening a doorway in the middle of the circle. The orb vanished.

In its place stood Katrina.

CHAPTER THIRTY-THREE

AT KATRINA'S APPEARANCE, I gasped. My mind raced through the possibilities. Was she a ghost? A vision? A memory? Or was she flesh and blood? Had the three of us actually brought Katrina, the real Katrina, into this room? She still wore the same outfit I'd seen when scrying her death in the mirror.

Although I'd known all along what we were trying to do, I'd never allowed myself to believe it might work. My heart squeezed with joy. I almost forgot that we were still in the middle of the spell.

At the sound of my gasp, Katrina turned, focusing her gaze on me. "Aly? What are you doing here?"

"Not now," Mary ordered. The strain of the magic was showing in her grimace. Sweat beaded on her forehead. She took the final corner of the fabric and held it out to her sister. "Walk toward me. Come through the doorway. Take this."

Although her nose wrinkled in confusion, Katrina took a step forward and grasped the fabric in one hand. She either trusted the three of us, or she was too confused to argue. Quickly, Mary handed me and Priscilla our squares. We unfolded the fabric to its full size, once again a flat sheet. The doorway full of light began to shrink.

Mary clapped. "So mote it be!"

The doorway vanished.

Katrina remained beside me.

That should have been the end of the spell, but something happened.

The room tilted. Everything swirled. My vision clouded. Pounding filled my ears. It felt like a massive head rush. All of a sudden, I was very grateful that we'd been sitting when we performed the spell. This must be what Mary meant. The world was changing around us.

Not wanting to disrupt the magic, I squeezed my eyes shut and waited. It felt like an eternity but was probably about two minutes. Then, finally, a stillness grew within me.

When I opened my eyes, I found myself sitting at a dark wooden table that had definitely seen better days. It wasn't the highly polished, gleaming mahogany in Kevin's dining room. Then again, this place also didn't have the damask wallpaper installed by Kevin's builder or the framed photos of Kyle and Katrina on the wall. Nothing but a blank, white wall stared back at me. Where was I?

The spell worked. It absolutely worked. But what did that mean for me? I didn't know where I was, but I wasn't in Kevin's house. Not the old one, not the one where we'd lived together for the past year.

Panic rose in my chest. I tamped it down by reciting the first fifteen elements. Everything would be okay. This was good news! If I were here, Katrina should be in her house, alive and well. I'd seen her. I'd *spoken* to her.

We'd actually done it. We'd saved her!

I needed to call Kevin. Well, he probably knew, since Katrina was in his house on an early Saturday morning. All she'd had to do was walk up the stairs. They must be reconnecting right now. He might not appreciate me interrupting.

That thought cheered me enough to return to my immediate problem: where was I?

The table in front of me held a variety of textbooks, all of which looked vaguely familiar but none of which I recalled owning. Stem Cell Biology, Recombinant DNA Technology, Biotechnology?

These were master's level courses, and I wouldn't finish my bachelor's degree for another few months. What was I doing? Did the books belong to someone else?

As I gazed around, I spotted a tablet lying on the other side of the table. A-ha! I grabbed it, hoping it would tell me something. Pressing a button on the front, I waited for it to light up and show me a background image.

Instead, a low-battery icon popped up. To be honest, that suggested it wasn't mine. I rarely left things like running out of power to chance. But that didn't tell me much. A quick survey of the room found a charger plugged into an outlet behind the chair against the far wall. Standing up, I scuffed my toes against the cheap beige carpet. As if I'd needed more proof that this wasn't Kevin's house. After attaching it, I pushed the power button a second time. Nothing. This thing was really dead. Better to leave it for a few minutes and come back.

I racked my brain, trying to figure out what was going on.

"Toto, I don't think we're in Kansas anymore," I said to no one as I walked around.

The table sat in a nook beside a small galley kitchen. It was perfectly functional, with a refrigerator, stove, and sink. Not much else. No dishwasher. No massive island where Kyle and I lovingly prepared food. No "mother's helper" stand where Kyle could climb up to see what I was working on and stick his fingers in the pancake batter.

I worried that meant my nephew didn't spend much time here.

The living room contained a couch, a chair, and a TV,

much like virtually every living room I'd ever been in. A *Star Wars* poster hung on one wall. Was I living here with Gabby?

Before moving to Shady Grove, I'd roomed with my long-time best friend. She loved all things science fiction and fantasy, but especially the *new Star Wars* trilogy. We'd been Rose and Rey for Halloween the year after the first one came out. When Katrina died, Gabby and I had shared a two-bedroom apartment not far from our community college. Was I still going there? It had been two years. I should have transferred to a four-year university by now, but that didn't mean we weren't still roomies. We could have moved to another building.

"Gabby?" I called, tentatively.

No one answered.

Through an opening between the dining area and the living room, I found a hall with three closed doors. The sound of running water reached me through the middle one. A-ha! I had a roommate, and she was taking a shower. Progress.

Since I couldn't talk to Gabby until she'd finished, I decided to see which bedroom belonged to me. First, to the right. I knocked, and no one answered.

Turning the knob, I pushed the door open.

Chaos greeted me. A tumble of green bedsheets. Clothes everywhere. A dresser with all kinds of crumpled papers and stuff on top. Although the sight probably should have alarmed me, it actually filled me with relief. This bedroom didn't look all that different from Gabby's space in our old apartment.

What had happened? Mary's spell pulled Katrina out of her house on that fateful day before she died, in the same spot now. If Katrina had been pulled from 2020 to 2022, then Katrina never died in 2020. If Katrina never died, she… disappeared? Mary would have shown up at the house to find her sister not there.

The Katrina we ripped from the past would be returned to

her foyer. Could Mary plan to be there, or had her world rearranged the way mine had?

My brain was still spinning, trying to figure out the potential ramifications, when my phone rang. Mary's name and face showed up on the display. Praise Newton. Apparently, in the reality we'd created, I had her number saved in my phone. I didn't even care why or how that happened.

But what if this Mary didn't know we'd done the spell? What if—?

My questions didn't matter at the moment. I needed to answer the phone before it went to voicemail. No time to plan what to say.

"Hi, Mary!" I said with false cheer.

"Aly." She sounded happy, but when she paused, her uncertainty filled the silence. "Where are you?"

"An excellent question," I said. "Some apartment somewhere."

As we spoke, I walked toward the window. Wherever I'd wound up, it was early December. About three seconds of cold air should tell me whether I was in the chilly northeast or the more temperate climate where I'd grown up.

"There's no good way to ask this," she said. "Do you remember the spell we just did?"

"There's no non-weird way to answer," I replied. "Yes, I do. Are you trying to tell me that Katrina's alive?"

Mary's relief was palpable. "She is! We're here together."

Sheer joy filled me. Never in my life had I felt such enormous relief. "Great! Where's here?"

"Star's Ridge. The old house. The house where you and I were with Priscilla about four minutes ago."

Thank goodness. Everything was starting to make sense. "We pulled her through that doorway. Did Katrina move forward in time?"

"She did. She's here with me. A little shaken, but alive. So alive."

My sister-in-law was back. The thought stopped me in my tracks, too overwhelmed to move.

"Aly?" All of a sudden, Katrina's voice filled my ear. I didn't even try to stop the tears of joy streaming down my face. "I understand that I have a lot to thank you for."

"Not at all," I said. "I'm so glad you're back. A little dazed, but thrilled. We've all missed you terribly."

She paused while someone spoke in the background. "Forgive me. It seems like I just saw Kevin and Kyle a few hours ago. But to them, I've been gone for years. My baby boy is so big now! I barely recognized him. I think I need to lie down."

"I understand. Give Kyle hugs for me."

"I'm never going to let him go."

She passed the phone back to Mary. "How do you feel, Aly?"

"Good? How are you?"

"I feel amazing, to be honest. Happier than I've felt in years."

Her tone made my ears perk up. This was not the voice of someone who was happier than she'd been in years. "What's wrong, Mary?"

"My magic is gone," she said.

"Sure. That was a huge spell. Anyone would be drained."

"No. Not drained. I can't explain how, but I can *feel* it. It's like, I got what I wanted. I got Katrina back. But there's a price. My magic was that price. Do you still have your powers?"

A chill went down my spine. No more powers? That wasn't part of the equation when we discussed what could happen. Not that it mattered. Katrina's life was worth so much more than a few visions, even if I tried to use them to help others when possible.

Closing my eyes, I reached inside myself. I focused my energy on the inner well where my powers normally lived. It was low, lower than I'd ever seen it. Of course, in this reality, I didn't know how much I'd trained with Olive. If I hadn't gotten a chance to grow my powers, maybe this was what they looked like.

"I think I'm okay," I said. "Drained, but there's something there. It should bounce back."

"We'll know when you have another vision, I guess. I can't thank you enough."

"And you don't need to. We're family." I looked around the apartment yet again. "But if you wanted to do something for me, you could answer a question. Where am I?"

"You're in the place you would be in 2022 if Katrina had lived. Imagine that she disappeared instead of dying. What would have happened in your life?"

"Wouldn't I still have moved to Shady Grove to help Kevin and Kyle?"

"You didn't need to. Kevin didn't want to move, because he wanted Katrina to find him when she returned. He never gave up hope that she would come home alive. They still own their house. On the day she disappeared, I had already been coming to visit. When I got here, my sister was missing. I called the police. I've been helping Kevin with Kyle ever since."

"They didn't need me." Weird how much those words punched me in the gut. Although I'd never planned to move in with my much older brother and help raise his child, in my world, it had happened. We'd become closer than I ever imagined, and the thought of not seeing Kyle's little face every day hurt.

Even though, of course, I was ecstatic that his mother was alive.

"They'll always need you, Aly. We're family. You're welcome here any time."

"What about school? Did I decide not to go to Maloney College?"

"You enrolled in Maloney to be near family. You drive to Kevin's every weekend to help. The two of you are very close, and Kyle adores you."

That made sense, at least. I was so relieved to hear that this spell hadn't ruined my relationship with my nephew. But something tickled the back of my mind.

"Do I have an apartment in Shady Grove? Who is my roommate?"

"You live in an apartment not far from campus, and you work at Missing Pieces two days a week."

Thank goodness for small favors. I still had Olive in my life. And Sam. I'd been so afraid I wouldn't know Sam anymore.

Somewhere to my left, a door slammed.

A male voice called out. "Hello? Anyone here?"

It wasn't Sam's voice. Did my roommate have a boyfriend? Or maybe I'd found a male roommate. Living with Rusty would be cool. Except he should be living with Doug, and that guy didn't sound like Rusty.

"Hello?" he called again.

If I wasn't going to answer him, I needed to leave. Something I couldn't do without shoes and my car keys. Assuming I owned a car.

"Mary? I'll have to call you back." The words were barely out of my mouth before I slid my phone into the side pocket of my leggings. At least my fashion sense hadn't changed.

"Aly? Is that you?"

Before I could respond, a red-headed stranger stepped into the doorway, his shoulders almost filling the doorframe. When he saw me, his face broke into a smile. His brown eyes crinkled at the corners. A smattering of freckles made him immediately look friendly. Good thing he didn't look threatening, since he wore only a towel wrapped around his waist.

I didn't have the faintest idea who he was.

My first instinct was to back away, but clearly this guy was a friend of mine. Or possibly my roommate.

As my brain whirled, trying to process everything that was happening, the guy stepped forward and cupped my face with both hands. Before I could even process what was happening, he kissed me. Warm lips pressed against mine, gently.

I stiffened.

Instantly, the guy let go. He took a step back, eyes searching mine. "What's wrong, Babe? You don't look happy to see me."

Oh, fluorine. Whatever else was happening in this universe, apparently I had a boyfriend. One who wasn't Sam.

Preorder now from your favorite retailer

relax with some family fun at the Shady Grove Annual Trea-sure Hunt. For twenty-five years, town residents have searched futilely for a chest containing the deed to an aban-doned mansion on the edge of town. At this point, Aly's pretty sure the treasure is a myth, but she's always up for Shady Grove shenanigans.

When the Treasure Hunt gets underway, a suspicious new resident throws everything into question. Someone's got a hidden motive for participating, and the town may be in danger. Can Aly solve the mystery to save the day?

MYSTIC TREASURE PREVIEW

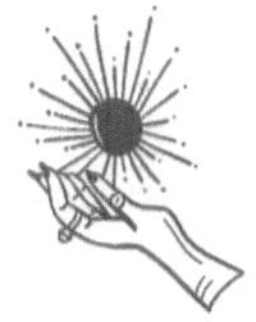

Today was the perfect day to win a fortune. I wasn't the only one who thought so: The Shady Grove Town Square hummed with excitement. Fluffy white cumulus clouds peppered the sky. Between the slight breeze and the mercury topping out at seventy degrees, this was the kind of gorgeous summer day that made it worth living through the humidity and thundershowers.

Half the town must have turned out to watch this event. Granted, half the town meant a few thousand people, but still. Town Square was bursting at the seams. Set near the end of Main Street, the largest park in town ran a block down to Second Street, with the other end across the street from City Hall. My three-year-old nephew and I stood under a tree, soaking it all in while we waited for my brother to join us.

Thankfully, Kyle hadn't yet seen the guy making balloon animals. On the corner nearest me, a marching band warmed up their instruments, complete with a bagpipes player. Town residents milled around, visiting the booths that had been set up to feed and entertain us. A huge banner extended across the square, welcoming everyone to the "WALTER SPARROW ANNUAL MEMORIAL TREASURE HUNT".

According to the rumor mill, Walter Sparrow was some eccentric millionaire who died about twenty-five years ago. Instead of leaving his money to a relative or a friend or a local animal shelter, he created this big annual party for everyone to try to win the big prize. No one had managed yet. My best friend Rusty suspected the entire story was a lie, and Walter just wanted to make sure we all talked about him forever after he passed.

Considering the amount of money supposedly on the line, I was surprised there weren't fortune hunters sniffing around all year, but Shady Grove wasn't like other towns. Maybe the same forces that led to unusual happenings kept outsiders away?

Or maybe our town was so tiny that no one outside a fifty-mile radius had heard of Shady Grove or old Walter? That was more likely.

Personally, I suspected Rusty was right. The whole thing sounded like an urban legend. An excuse for a big summer party, but anyone expecting to find treasure would be sorely disappointed. Still, we'd teamed up and gotten ready for action. The practice solving clues should come in handy once Rusty finished getting his PI license.

Tugging my hand, Kyle peered up at me with his big brown eyes and heart-shaped face from beneath his adorably oversized sun hat. "What's a treasure hunt, Aunt Aly?"

I resisted smoothing an errant chestnut curl that was so like mine. "It means Rusty and I are going to follow clues to find a lost item that has been hidden somewhere in the town."

"I find it! What did Rusty lose?" Kyle asked.

I grinned at the spark of excitement in his eyes and smoothed a curl off of his forehead. My nephew had been born with the power to find lost objects, a secret we preferred to keep from the rest of the world as long as possible. Psychic powers ran in our family, but we'd recently learned that some people wanted to exploit what he could do. "Thanks, Little Man, but this game is for adults only. Besides, in a game, it's not fair to use our special abilities to win."

"Cheating?"

"Yes, that's considered cheating."

"Oh. I won't cheat." Kyle stuck out his lower lip. Then his gaze landed on one of the tables below the "WALTER SPARROW MEMORIAL TREASURE HUNT" banner. "Cookie?"

With a laugh, I let him drag me to the table, manned by my friend and the owner of the local coffee shop, Julie Capaldi. A self-described "recovering lawyer," Julie was a blue-eyed blonde who'd moved to Shady Grove a few years ago to take over her aunt's business. She'd set out cookies for sale, but also—and more importantly—iced coffee.

"Hey! Looking forward to the hunt?" she asked when we got within earshot.

"You know it," I said. "Rusty's excited to practice his PI skills. I'm here to stop him from picking the locks of every store on Main Street."

She laughed. "He's going to be a great investigator. I miss having him at the cafe, though."

Until recently, Rusty had worked as the manager at On What Grounds?. After helping me learn to use my powers and solve a murder, my new best friend discovered his true calling. I often considered myself fortunate Julie hadn't banned me from her store when he left. Where would I get my coffee?

Then again, I suspected she had a thing for my brother.

"Hey, kiddo!" she said to Kyle before offering him a cookie. "You planning to hunt treasure today?"

"Aunt Aly said I was cheating."

My face flamed. Maybe she wouldn't understand him?

Three-year-olds didn't have the best enunciation, and his mouth was full of cookie. I wasn't sure how much Julie knew, either about Kyle's abilities or mine. She certainly hadn't heard it from me, but small towns didn't have many secrets.

"Cheating? That's no good." She gave me one of those 'kids say the darnedest things' grins.

In response, I gave her the most innocent look I could muster. "We're learning new words this week. Anyway, are you entering?"

"No, I can't."

"Can't?"

She shook her head and laughed. "I did it last year. You're only allowed to enter once."

"That's odd," I said. "Kevin did it last year, too. I thought he wasn't entering because he wanted to spend the day with Kyle."

"That's part of it, I'm sure. But yeah, everyone gets one chance." She shrugged. "People with money are eccentric, right? It's Walter's estate, so he gets to make the rules. I'll send all my good vibes to you and Rusty."

At the mention of my partner, I turned to scan the crowd. With the pre-hunt festivities drawing to an end, Town Square had cleared out somewhat. A lot of people still stood around, but most moved to ring the center, where the hunt would soon begin.

About fifteen feet away, I spotted my friend Tiffaneigh Pratt talking to Brad Stevens. The three of us studied science together at Maloney College. She still didn't want to admit they were dating, but the two of them looked awfully cozy. Their matching bright blue shirts with "WALTER SPARROW HUNTER" on the back told me everything I needed to know about their relationship—and my primary competition. Tiffaneigh hated to lose, and she had some flexible ideas about what constituted fair and legal gameplay.

We'd need to keep an eye on her if we wanted to win.

Mystic Treasure is ONLY available by signing up for my newsletter - visit www.adabell.com to get your copy.

ABOUT THE AUTHOR

Ada Bell is an award-winning and internationally best-selling author who thought that it would be cool to use a secret identity when writing mysteries. After all, who doesn't want a secret identity? She doesn't remember where the idea for the Shady Grove mysteries started, but she freely admits that Kyle is based on a certain precious toddler in her own life. Ada loves Scooby Doo, superhero movies, STEM heroines, and cake. Mmm, cake.

Find Ada online at www.adabell.com, or get access to sneak peeks, news and more by joining her Facebook group or mailing list.

AUTHOR'S NOTE

SPOILERS AHEAD. If you somehow came to this author's note without reading the full book, this is your only warning. Go back to the beginning. Start with page 1. Enjoy. And don't let me ruin the ending for you. (The ending is pretty good—you want to experience it yourself.)

Funny thing... This book came about from a game I was playing. I've always been a fan of the "Groundhog Day" trope because the idea of getting to repeat things until you get it right appeals to me. Sometimes it feels like every sci-fi or fantasy series has the obligatory time loop episode: Star Trek, Stargate, Xena, Buffy... (Why, yes, I have watched all of those.) But I hadn't really planned in advance to do one.

I was playing Elsinore. It's a computer game where the player is living in Hamlet as Ophelia, trying to avoid the tragic events of the play. It's an interesting game. And I was absolutely adoring it...until I managed to put myself in an unwinnable state. Rather than resetting and beginning from zero, I decided to channel my frustration into my work in progress. And—ta da! Here we are. :-)

From the beginning, I always intended to find a way to bring Katrina back. I never had any idea how to achieve this goal. Obviously, Aly couldn't loop back to the day her sister-in-law died. That would be two years, and that made no sense. But once the idea of a time loop came into play, I realized that one of Shady Grove's powerful witches was going to have to appear. And then I realized I had my work cut out for me rehabilitating Mary. I hope you like the result.

Writing has always been a comfort to me, but I actually started this series because I needed a change. My romcoms were bringing me down, and I was having trouble writing about love and hope in a Covid-central world. But in switching gears, in hearing how people have responded to Aly, I have found what I need. Thank you for reading this series. I appreciate you more than you can know, and I'm excited to keep it going as long as I can.

A SHADY GROVE CHRONOLOGY

<u>Mystic Pieces:</u> Aly doesn't believe in psychics. Too bad she just had her first vision. Her first instinct is flat-out denial. After all, science and magic don't mix. But when a man is murdered, Aly realizes that she may be able to use her strange new "gifts" to find the culprit. If she can avoid getting herself killed in the process.

<u>The Scry's the Limit</u>: Aly's just starting to get the hang of her psychic gifts when she literally stumbles over her favorite professor's body. She's devastated and determined to get justice. But with several people benefitting from Professor Zimm's death, how will Aly find the real culprit before they find her?

<u>Sight Seering</u>: As a psychic who gains powers from antiques, Aly is ecstatic to be invited to an estate sale. It's only after she

arrives that she discovers the estate's owner didn't die in her sleep—she was murdered.

<u>Mystic Treasure</u>: Aly and Rusty are excited to participate in the annual Walter Sparrow Treasure Hunt. As the event gets underway, they realize that there's more to this event than meets the eye. Someone's got a hidden motive for participating, and the entire town may be in danger.

This novella takes place between the final chapters and epilogue of *Sight Seering*. *Mystic Treasure* is ONLY available by signing up for my newsletter at www.adabell.com. Thank you for hanging out with me!

<u>Seer Today, Gone Tomorrow</u>: Just when Aly finally identified her sister-in-law's killer, they got away—and they're not alone. To make matters worse, someone powerful has cursed the residents of Shady Grove. Aly's powers vanish. Without her psychic gifts, how will Aly find Katrina's killer and save the pet store?

<u>The Pie in the Scry</u>: After nearly a year, Aly's got a plan to bring Katrina's killer to justice. But before she and Kevin can implement it, she has a vision of someone murdering Tony, the bakery owner. As if that wasn't bad enough—the killer looks exactly like Aly.

<u>Mystic Persons</u>: Aly just completed the biggest spell she's ever attempted, with a little help. But the magic came with an unexpected side effect, and now she's got to figure out what happened to the dead man in the upstairs bath before her parents arrive for the holidays.

HAUNTED HAVEN SERIES

EMMA THOUGHT life was weird before she found out she was a witch. Now she's got some pretty cool powers, a snarky-yet-insightful talking cat, and a fabulous mansion-turned-B&B, complete with ghost. Here is your complete guide to the *Haunted Haven* series.

Unfinished Witchness: Emma is thrilled to come into her legacy: not only has she inherited stacks of money and a mansion, she's got magic! Everything is coming up roses until she finds her new chef dead in the kitchen and her other employee accused of murder. If she can't find the real killer, this haunted haven might never open for business.

Risky Witchness: Now that Emma's bed and breakfast is bustling with activity, she decides to treat herself to some R&R at the local fancy spa. But when she finds another guest dead, Emma becomes the prime suspect. She'll need the help of his ghost to help find the real killer before they find her.

<u>Open for Witchness:</u> When Ben convinces Emma to investigate the mysteriously closed bar in Shady Grove, she discovers it's being guarded by an extremely unpleasant spirit. The only way to help her friend is to solve the mystery —but the trail has been cold for decades. Can she close the case and reopen the bar?

WRITTEN AS LAURA HEFFERNAN

Retail to Riches Series

A Royal Farce: After years of secretly crushing on her friend Pierre, Lila is thrilled when he proposes they start a fake relationship. For weeks, she finds herself hoping their farce could turn into the real thing—but Pierre's hiding a secret of royal magnitude.

A Royal Pain: When Lila and Pierre arrive in Corchenne to meet her in-laws, she's shocked to discover that her scheming brother has already arrived. Can their marriage survive Caleb's shenanigans and the weight of royal expectations?

The Reality Star Series

America's Next Reality Star: Jen went on a reality show to compete for the $250,000 grand prize. But when she finds herself battling another woman for co-competitor Justin's heart, she finds herself wondering what the true prize is.

Sweet Reality: After a killer competitor threatens her new business, Jen sets sail on a new reality show adventure to save the day. But Ariana's back, and she's determined to end Jen and Justin's relationship once and for all.

Reality Wedding: After retiring from reality TV, Jen receives an offer she can't refuse. The Network wants Jen and Justin to film their wedding to fill an empty time slot—and if they refuse, the Network will get Justin fired.

The Gamer Girls Series

She's Got Game: Gwen's dedicated to becoming the American Board Games Champion, and she never ever mixes gaming with pleasure.

But when she meets Cody, trying to resist his charm becomes a losing proposition.

Against the Rules: For years, Holly has harbored a secret crush on her best friend's dad. Nathan is young, he's hot. What's a little harmless flirtation while playing games? But when she discovers that Nathan returns her feelings, Holly may have to choose between two of the most important people in her life.

Make Your Move: Shannon's more interested in designing games and rising to the top at work than dating. She's surprised to find herself falling for her roommate, Tyler. Worse, he's dating her boss's daughter. If she makes her move, Tyler's girlfriend could get Shannon fired.

Push and Pole Series

Poll Dancer: A delightfully modern twist on *My Fair Lady*: When a promotional video for her pole-dancing classes goes viral, Mel comes under fire from a local politician running for senate. Desperate to save her studio, Mel decides her only option is to launch her own campaign — and win!

The Accidental Senator: After accidentally finding herself elected state senator, Lana Chen is determined to prove her worth. But when a mistake aids the passage of a bill that's going to put her best friend out of business, Lana has to find a way to set things right before it's too late.

Standalone Books

Finding Tranquility: Christa Cooper finds the courage to transition after she nearly loses her life on September 11. Eighteen years later, she's confronted by the wife she left behind: Jess, who discovers that the person she knew as Brett is now Christa. Can they find a future together, despite the past?

Anna's Guide to Getting Even: Anna's perfect life has turned into a string of disasters: After a hurricane destroys her house, her ex publicizes private photos of her — which costs Anna her job and her current boyfriend. And after hitting rock bottom, she decides that revenge is the only way forward…

Friction: Britt's always avoided relationships. Then, weeks before she's set to move away, she meets Colin. To her surprise, she finds herself wanting more.